THE NIGHT ANGELS

The Secret Sirens Series
Book Two

D. R. Bailey

SAPERE
BOOKS

THE NIGHT ANGELS

Published by Sapere Books.

24 Trafalgar Road, Ilkley, LS29 8HH

saperebooks.com

ISBN: 978-0-85495-641-8

I would like to dedicate this book to my eldest sister, Catharine Bird. Cathy, an artist, has had a huge influence on my writing aspirations, from telling me amazing stories as a child, to introducing me to her vast library of science fiction novels as a teenager. She has always been supportive of everything I've done and this dedication is a way of saying thank you, for everything, with all my love.

CHAPTER ONE

March 1943
Northern France

"Wigwam in five," said Assistant Section Officer Maria Preston, my navigator, referring to the codename for the target.

"Roger," I replied.

I banked the Mosquito as she gave out the bearing which would take the flight directly over the target. Our mission was part of Operation Scorpion, a series of hit-and-run raids on airbases in northern France. It was a dark night, but we were all used to night flying now. We'd had enough training during the six months we had been stationed at Hawberry Hall.

"Panthers, prepare to attack," I radioed the other two Mosquitos. Panther Six was piloted by Section Officer Susan Bell, with Assistant Section Officer Pamela Hartley navigating. Their plane was fitted with air-to-air radar, one of two in the squadron with this equipment. As a result, they got to fly more raids than the rest of us. Panther Two was flown by Section Officer Patricia Batley, with Assistant Section Officer Connie Broadbent as navigator.

"There it is," said Maria.

Sure enough, the airbase hove into view. We were skimming treetops and hedge-hopping — dropping low and then hopping up and over obstacles. It was scary stuff, but to some extent, we had become inured to it.

The cockpits of the planes on the ground glinted in the moonlight. We had been informed that the airbase housed a fighter squadron. Our mission was simply to strafe the airfield, drop ordnance and get out in short order.

"Any bandits, Panther Six?" I asked, since Pamela would be watching the radar like a hawk. It was her duty to detect enemy incursions or threats.

"Negative," came the response.

That was good news; Jerry had nothing airborne in our vicinity. We'd hopefully take them by surprise.

"Let's do this. Fire at will," I said, slipping off the safety catch on the guns.

We barrelled in fast and low, following the path of the runway. The German planes were nicely lined up for us like sitting ducks. The cannons from three Mosquitos tore up the dirt. There was a series of explosions as the ammo hit the planes and they immediately caught fire.

"Searchlights!" shouted Maria as the powerful lights split the night sky, trying to seek us out.

"Watch those lights, Panthers, drop and go," I said, banking sharply towards the buildings. We still had to drop our ordnance in order to cause more damage.

Tracers streamed out from machine gun emplacements, trying to draw a bead on us. We neatly avoided the incoming fire and the searchlights, either by luck or good judgement. The other two Mosquitos dropped their bombs over the hangars and sped on to the rendezvous.

"What about us?" asked Maria, flicking a glance at me as I still hadn't dropped ours.

"We're taking the control tower," I replied, having made a spur-of-the-moment decision.

"Oh God, here we go again," she said with resignation as the tower loomed up in front of us. Streams of tracers shot past the canopy, but I kept the plane on target.

"I hope you know what you're doing, Anna," said Maria.

"Not really," I quipped. "But I thought it was worth a shot."

"I figured as much," she shot back with a hollow laugh.

I opened the bomb bay doors and at the last moment banked sharply, exposing the underbelly of the plane to the tower. We were going to pass it at quite a lick, and I was relying on the momentum of the plane.

"Bombs away," I said, releasing our deadly payload.

If I was right, they would fly straight into the tower building and blow it up, kind of like a catapult. Taking down the tower would be quite a disruption. I turned the plane away and opened up the throttle to get clear. Seconds later, I had the satisfaction of seeing a big explosion lighting up the tower before it keeled over.

"Can we get the hell out of here now, please?" said Maria.

"That's no way to talk to a senior officer," I said, laughing.

"Can we get the hell out of here now, please, ma'am," she said, laughing too.

In high spirits, we headed for the rendezvous point. So far so good; this was turning into another successful mission. When we arrived, I radioed the rest of the flight.

"Panthers, we're at the Band Stand."

The Band Stand was the rendezvous codename; the other two Mosquitos would have circled around waiting for us to arrive.

"Roger," said Patricia. "We've got you."

"Panthers, form up on me."

The two Mosquitos settled in formation, one on each side of my wings.

"I think you're enjoying this war stuff a bit too much," said Maria as she set a bearing back to Hawberry.

"Perhaps I am…"

I throttled up and dropped down as low as I could. Then it was up and over hedges, houses, trees, telegraph lines, running for the coast. In spite of my apparent flippancy, I was well aware of the danger we were in while over hostile territory.

As we flew north, the familiar hazard-spotting routine kicked in as the terrain flashed by.

"Trees," said Maria

"Seen them."

"Lines."

"Got them."

"House."

"Yep."

I hopped up and over just as we'd done countless times before. It had become second nature. Even so, one wrong move could cost us our lives. We also knew that as members of the Sirens we either returned to Blighty in one piece, or died in the attempt. There were no other options for us. We were one of the best-kept secrets of the war — a squadron of female pilots whose existence would never be officially acknowledged by the British command. Like our mythological namesakes, we were deadly shadows, striking down the enemy and disappearing back into the night as if we had never been.

So far, we'd been successful, having lost only one plane and crew. I hoped our luck would hold.

"Coast in ten," said Maria.

I breathed a sigh of relief, glad to leave the coast of France behind.

"Radar contact," said Pamela suddenly.

"Bandits?" I asked her.

"Hard to tell, but we're closing fast."

It would be just our luck to run into enemy aircraft on the way home. I slipped the safety catch off once more.

"Keep your eyes peeled," I said.

"It's just one, I think," said Pamela.

That, at least, gave us better odds. I started scanning the skies ahead for a glimpse of an aircraft when Patricia shouted out a warning.

"There he is, twelve o'clock, dead ahead!"

Indeed, there it was in the distance — the gleam of a single aircraft. We could see some visible flare from the exhausts on the engines.

"He's coming straight for us," said Patricia.

"Engage as soon as he's in range," I ordered.

"Looks like an Me 110," said Susan.

The Messerschmitt Bf 110 was a twin-engine fighter. The Germans used them as night fighters. Since we'd been attacking their airbases with such ferocity, they had started deploying them. So far, we had evaded them. This time we'd been caught.

Agonising seconds passed as the 110 kept coming.

Suddenly a stream of tracers erupted from Patricia's plane. As soon as I saw this, I opened fire too. A third burst appeared from Susan's Mosquito. The 110 returned fire, but then I saw one of its engines start to flame.

"We've hit it," cried Patricia with some jubilation.

The enemy plane twisted sideways as the engine exploded. Behind us, it started to dive to earth as we kept going.

We crossed the French coastline and flew over the black water of the Channel. The majestic chalk cliffs of Beachy Head loomed up before us. I took us higher and then we were safely over British territory once more.

I breathed a sigh of relief. All I had to do now was get us home. As we flew on through the night, still keeping low, my mind wandered a little.

Wing Commander James Donnington was the CO of the Sirens. Following our raid on the Carlingue secret prison the previous year, we had entered into a tenuous relationship. One very long kiss had sealed the deal, and ever since we had kept our clandestine meetings secret.

I was just recalling that kiss when a loud voice jerked me back to the present.

"Anna, what the hell are you doing?" shouted Maria.

I realised that we very low; so low, in fact, that the Mosquito was almost slicing the daisies in a field. Dead ahead were telegraph poles and lines. We were too close to pull up. I had no choice but to fly under the wires.

I kept the kite steady. It was not for nothing that I'd pulled some extremely dangerous stunts in a Tiger Moth back home on my father's farm in Sussex. Still, my heart was in my mouth as we safely passed under the wires.

As we emerged on the other side, I pulled up on the stick. I took us higher and out of harm's way.

"See," I said. "All under control."

"That's what you call it, is it?" said Maria. "I thought those were my last moments on God's green earth."

"Nice circus trick, Panther Leader," said Patricia.

"I'm doing my best to keep you entertained, Panther Two."

"Don't encourage her," Maria told Patricia.

I refrained from making another quip as the familiar sight of Hawberry Hall and the airfield came into view. We lined up for the approach one by one, with our plane going first.

"Control, this is Panther Leader requesting permission to land."

"Roger, Panther Leader, you're clear," came the response from Control.

"Three Panthers returning intact," I said as the runway lights came on.

"Roger, well done."

One by one we landed and taxied to our designated standings. I applied the brakes and the Mosquito came to a stop.

"Thank God for that," said Maria as I killed the engines. "I've had more than enough excitement for one night."

I laughed and reached over to squeeze her hand.

"Sorry," I said. "For being distracted."

"What were you thinking about?" Maria asked. "As if I didn't know."

There was no point in lying or prevaricating. Not much got past her. The Sirens had become a tight-knit team, but Maria and I were particularly close. Only my sister, Section Officer Jennifer Nightingale, was closer still.

"You guessed right," I said, without mentioning James by name.

"You're in love with him, aren't you?" Maria said perceptively.

I shook my head. "I can't be in love with him; I'm the Flight Leader, I have responsibilities."

"Oh? You think the two are mutually exclusive?"

I sighed. Maria could be persistent, and often annoyingly right.

"I don't know what to think."

"What *I* think is that you need to keep your mind on the job — at least when you're flying, because I want to survive this war."

She was smiling as she said it; however, I pounced on this at once.

"There, you see — you've just proved my point," I said triumphantly.

"And you can have a relationship too. You'll work it out, Anna."

Just then there was a sudden banging on the side door and a voice called, "What are you two doing in there?"

It was Assistant Section Officer Shelly Cartwright. She and Maria were from the same village in Wales and had grown up together. Shelly had got herself into one or two scrapes during her time in the Sirens, much to Maria's annoyance.

"Come on, Boss, let's go," said Maria.

Boss was the nickname that Shelly had started giving me. Everyone had now picked up on it and it had stuck.

I sighed and Maria shot me an affectionate smile. In the end, I was going to have to work the James thing out for myself. We unstrapped and then Maria opened the door and we jumped down to the ground.

"What are you doing here?" Maria asked Shelly. "You're not on duty."

"Came to see how you got on," said Shelly. Then she shot us a sly look. "Also, Jennifer wanted to see Connie."

I realised that was the real reason as soon as I saw Jennifer and Connie standing next to each other, sharing a cigarette. Jennifer's blonde hair contrasted with Connie's red locks in the lights from the hangars. The ground crew was already swinging into action to see to the planes.

Shelly sniggered and I said nothing. Jennifer and Connie were more than just friends. I had seen them kiss once in the gardens of Hawberry Hall. We had never really discussed their relationship, but in the end, it was Jennifer's business, not mine. Within the confines of the Sirens, they would be relatively safe from public scrutiny.

"Are we going back to the Hall or what?" demanded Patricia. "For one thing I'm hungry, and for another, it's bloody cold out here."

In spite of our warm clothing, the air was certainly chilly. It was highly likely a frost would set in as the night was clear. Winter hadn't quite released us from its grip, even though it was purportedly spring.

"Come on," I said and then called out to Jennifer. "Let's go, Jenny."

"Hey, you two, stop dawdling, the Boss has spoken," said Shelly.

We piled into the back of the waiting truck. It trundled back to Hawberry Hall, an impressive three-storey manor house set in well landscaped grounds barely a mile from the airfield and hangars. The whole place was assiduously guarded and off-limits to everyone except those who had business with the Sirens and the Sirens personnel.

Connie and Jennifer sat at the back of the truck, sharing a cigarette and blowing the smoke out of the opening.

"Your sister did some stunt flying tonight," said Patricia mendaciously.

Jennifer perked up at once. "Oh? Do tell."

"Yeah, she flew right under some telegraph wires… It was most impressive," Paticia continued.

"I'm glad the rest of you didn't follow me," I remarked.

"Thought about it," Susan put in and we all laughed. Susan had turned out to be game for some pretty outrageous shenanigans.

"Anna could always pull off the most dangerous stunts at our father's flying displays, so I'm not surprised," said Jennifer, taking another drag on her cigarette.

The two of us had been stunt pilots with Nightingale's Flying Circus, a highly successful show, until we'd both been recruited to the Sirens.

"Well, I'm glad you're all back safe," said Connie, putting an end to the topic, much to my relief.

As always after a mission, refreshments had been laid on in the dining room. James, however, was not present. His absence irked me. Didn't he care that we had just returned from a dangerous mission? I wondered if I should go to his room. But I was pretty tired, and it was late, so I decided to go to bed. Jennifer joined me after taking a midnight walk with Connie. Our room had a double and a single bed, but we preferred to snuggle up together, just like when we were children.

CHAPTER TWO

Breakfast the following morning was the usual boisterous affair. I tucked into the ubiquitous fare of toast, eggs and baked beans at our usual table. Occasionally we'd get some bacon or sausages. Generally, rations were good. I sipped my tea and looked around. James was seated at a table at the other end of the dining room with his adjutant Flight Sergeant Judy Royston, Wing Officer Gloria Shepherd, his deputy, and Flight Lieutenant Henry Peterson, who was one of our flight instructors. He flicked a glance at me but only gave a slight smile.

"Penny for your thoughts?" murmured Maria, who was sitting next to me.

"They're not worth a penny," I said, taking another sip of tea.

"He cares, even if you think he doesn't," she murmured.

"If you say so."

"I do, so stop worrying."

I nodded and addressed myself to my eggs once again.

"Who's worrying?" said Shelly, who never missed a trick.

"Nobody, but you should be, as you're next up for a mission," Maria shot back, successfully turning the subject.

"How long are we going to keep doing this Operation Scorpion?" said Connie.

"We do it for as long as we're ordered to do it," I said.

"The Boss has spoken," Shelly piped up at once.

"Honestly, Shelly, you really are..." I said, trying to think of the words.

"A damn hot navigator, and I can work the radar like a dream," Shelly finished for me, unabashed.

"That's true," said Jennifer. "She can."

"And who's the man of the moment this week, Shelly?" asked Pamela, referring to Shelly's well-deserved reputation with a number of the male personnel.

"Nobody."

"Oh, sure, of course..." said Maria in disbelieving tones.

I tuned out of the conversation as I concentrated on my breakfast. Ordinarily, I would have joined in with the banter, but I was feeling somewhat distracted.

With breakfast over, we filed into the room where we had all our briefings. Chairs were set out in rows facing one end of the room, which had a slightly raised podium. There was a large map of Europe on the wall and a projector screen which could be pulled down. It was used to project reconnaissance photographs, though we sometimes used it to watch films as part of the in-house entertainment.

Because I was Flight Leader and a senior officer, I insisted on sitting at the front, much to Shelly's annoyance, who liked to sit at the back.

James, Gloria and Henry arrived in short order. We all stood to attention as they entered the room and took their place on the podium.

"At ease," said James in his usual affable manner.

We seated ourselves and waited to hear what might be in store. Briefings were less common now that Operation Scorpion was up and running, and we had also become an experienced team.

"Some time ago," James began, "I promised that the Sirens would be augmented by new pilots and navigators. It's taken a while to organise and find suitable candidates. However, I'm pleased to tell you that we are about to be joined by a new cohort to beef up the squadron."

This pronouncement brought a buzz of excitement to the room.

"This is quite a coup," James continued. "It means that the higher-ups have recognised our worth. They're willing to invest a little bit more in this unit because we're doing a damn fine job."

"Are we going to keep flying these Scorpion missions, sir?" Shelly piped up.

Maria tried to shush her, but James wasn't in the least bit fazed by the question.

"For the moment, yes, but you will also be involved in training the new crew, settling them in, that sort of thing."

There were a few murmurs at this; I wasn't sure if the mutterings sounded a little like dissent. I supposed it was understandable now that we'd become a tight-knit team to view the newcomers as outsiders.

"I am sure you'll be eager to assist in helping the new members become part of the squadron," James continued. "Is that not so, Flight Officer Nightingale?"

I felt a flush rising to my face. He had put me on the spot. I had realised very soon after becoming Flight Leader that I had to step up to the position. However, that didn't mean I liked talking to large groups of people, particularly when I didn't know it was coming. Nevertheless, I stood up and turned to face the crew.

"The Wing Commander is right," I said, thinking on my feet. "We were all new once, and we shouldn't forget that. I expect everyone here to do their duty in that regard. I take it as a compliment that we're getting new people. It shows we're doing a good job." I started to warm to my theme. "Just think about that — we are the only female combat unit in the country. Let's show the newcomers a proper Siren's welcome and take them into our fold. What do you say?"

A moment later, the rest of the squadron were on their feet and cheering. All bar one. Noticeably silent and evidently still harbouring resentment against me was SO Linda Harris. It seemed she could not get over the fact that I had been appointed Flight Leader and not her. I glanced at James. He had noticed it too.

"All right, all right, settle down," said James, laughing at the raucous reaction.

As silence was once more restored, Shelly winked at me and resumed her seat.

"Thank you, FO Nightingale. Well, as your Flight Leader has so articulately stated, please do make your new colleagues feel at home."

"They will, of course, be going through the usual drill, flight training and more," added Gloria. "Just in case you were wondering."

There were a few sniggers at this. Drill was nobody's favourite activity.

Henry stepped forward on the podium. "For training purposes, we will be asking pilots and navigators to take out the newbies, so that they can fly with experienced personnel and get up to speed faster. We will, naturally, be encouraging them to pair off between themselves, just as you did."

This made perfect sense. I wondered if there might be some changes in crews over time. It seemed unlikely, because each team was used to each other by now. I certainly wouldn't want to lose Maria. Of course, if a team member was killed, that was a different matter. I didn't like to think about that; none of us did.

"Are there any questions?" said James.

There were none, and we were duly dismissed. James left the podium, along with Gloria and Henry. The room became a hubbub of noise. We had no particular exercises for the day so I decided to get some fresh air.

I was walking towards the front door of the Hall when Judy intercepted me.

"The CO would like to see you in his office, ma'am," she said, flicking me a salute.

"Of course," I said, returning the salute.

I wondered if Judy knew about my relationship with James. I'd have been surprised if she didn't, as she was his adjutant, but I knew she would never let on. She was privy to many secrets in her position and duty-bound to keep them. Besides which, she was fiercely loyal to James.

I accompanied Judy up the stairs and along various corridors to the familiar sitting-room-cum-office where James resided. Judy knocked, then stood aside to let me enter before closing the door behind me. The room was furnished with easy chairs and a sofa, along with a meeting table and a desk at one end where James was seated. The CO of the Sirens was in his mid-thirties, with black hair, a moustache, and brown eyes. I had always thought him handsome. He stood up at once and came towards me.

"There you are," he said, smiling.

"As you perceive," I replied.

"You didn't come and see me last night," he said in a teasing tone as he came forward to meet me.

"You weren't in the dining room to welcome me back," I shot back.

James ignored this somewhat petulant remark. I was in his arms before I knew it and it felt natural to be there. He kissed me and my stomach started doing flips, just as it always did when we were in close proximity. However, the doubts I'd been carrying began to find voice once he relaxed his hold on me, though I was feeling somewhat breathless.

"James, you can't … we can't…" I said.

"Can't what? Kiss you?" he asked, his eyes twinkling.

"Well, yes, you can, but how can we possibly be together? You're my boss."

James made light of it, although he had respected my desire for discretion.

"But we are together, aren't we?" he said. "Isn't that what we've been doing?"

"Well, yes, but … oh, it's not funny, James," I said, a little exasperated.

"We can work it out, I'm sure," he said in a more serious tone.

Upon which our lips met once more, and we lingered in another kiss. I managed to pull away at length and against my own will to continue.

"I can't think when you're doing that."

"Shall I stop?" he said, sounding amused.

"Yes … no … oh, I don't know." I slipped out of his grasp and stood a pace or two away from temptation.

"What do you want, Anna?" he asked gently.

"I want to keep flying and leading the flight," I said. My biggest fear was losing the position I'd won. I liked being Flight Leader and I did not want to relinquish the role.

"And you will." James shrugged as if it wasn't something I needed to be concerned about.

"But…" I tried again.

"You're worried about what the others will think?"

James filled in the blanks. I was sure he understood my sentiments already, but we'd never discussed it fully. I'd asked him not to make our relationship public and he'd agreed without argument. But we had to talk about it if we were ever to move forward.

"Yes."

"Does it matter so much?"

"It does to me."

James was silent for a moment.

"Then we won't say anything."

This wasn't entirely the answer I wanted, but I had no answers either. I didn't know how we could deal with the situation in a satisfactory way.

"What if someone finds out?" I asked him.

"Well, then we'll deal with that if it arises," he said, smiling.

"All right."

"You worry too much, my darling," he said softly.

"Is that a fact?"

I was in his arms once more, but this time it was me who had gone to him. I wound my arms around his neck.

"Yes, it is," he whispered. His lips were a hairsbreadth from mine.

I put aside my scruples and surrendered to another kiss.

CHAPTER THREE

Sandra Brown was something of an American bombshell. She arrived at Hawberry Hall along with eleven other women who were also joining the Sirens. James introduced them all at breakfast one day, not long after his recent announcement.

"If I could have your attention, please," he said, standing up and calling for hush by tapping a spoon on an empty china mug.

The dining room, which was normally rather loud, fell silent. I noticed Sergeant Martha Pryde, who had greeted us when we'd first arrived at Hawberry, standing with the group of newcomers, who were all in uniform.

"Thank you," said James. "I'd like to introduce our new recruits, or better still, they can shortly introduce themselves. We have twelve new additions to our squadron, and, as you can see, they've already been inducted. They will undergo intensive training over the next few weeks before flying missions."

To my irritation, James then singled me out as the Flight Leader. It was inevitable, of course, but I was still getting used to some of the exigencies of my duties.

"If Flight Officer Nightingale might stand up," he said, looking at me directly. "Anna is our Flight Leader. You can make yourself known to her. She's also colloquially known as the 'Boss' by the rest of the squadron."

There was some laughter at this. I had discovered some time ago that not much escaped James's notice.

"Anyway," he said, "I won't let the food get cold any longer. Make yourselves at home, and say hello to the others. After breakfast there will be a formal briefing. Thank you."

James sat down while I found myself assailed by one new recruit after another. I realised I would have to try and remember all their names.

Sandra breezed over and saluted in a slightly laconic fashion. She was extremely pretty, with blonde hair and blue eyes. She reminded me of one of those classic American pin-up girls.

"Hi," she said with a slight Southern drawl. "I'm Sandra Brown ... erm ... ma'am. I believe that's how I should address you."

"Hi, Sandra, welcome to the Sirens," I said, smiling. I held out my hand and she shook it.

"You can call her Boss," said Maria, cutting in. "I'm Maria, Anna's navigator."

"Pleased to meet you all," said Sandra, looking around the table. "Do you mind if I sit with you?"

"By all means," I said.

"I'll show you where to get some grub," said Shelly, taking her in hand at once.

As they departed, my attention was taken up once more by the new members who introduced themselves in turn and then took a seat at the various tables after obtaining some breakfast.

My own eggs on toast were lukewarm by the time Sandra returned to our table. She sat down with a goodly portion on her plate.

"Oh, don't mind me," she said breezily. "I always did have a healthy appetite."

"You're from America then, Sandra?" said Connie, rather stating the obvious.

"Yes, all the way from the US of A and proud of it." She noticed our expressions at this statement and added, "Of course, I'm also proud to be here and fighting with you British for the cause of freedom."

I let her tuck into her food before asking the obvious question.

"So, you're a pilot?" I said at length, pushing my now empty plate away.

"Yes, that's right. My daddy runs a flying circus — The Boston Barnstormers. I've been flying since I was little," Sandra said with a smile.

"My father does as well; that's how I caught the bug," I said.

"Here in England?" Sandra asked, and I nodded. "I was from Virginia originally, but my Daddy moved us out to Boston and that's where we stayed. But we did shows all over the country."

"How did you get picked to join the Sirens?" asked Susan.

"Oh, well, these two strange gentlemen came to see me, asked if I wanted to help the war effort over here. I was already flying with the Women's Auxiliary Ferrying Squadron, transporting planes."

I assumed that she meant the two spies from MI6, who we called the Marx Brothers. They had recruited all of us and were instrumental in the ongoing operations of the Sirens. The Marx Brothers had obviously spread their net far and wide in order to find the best people for the Sirens, and Sandra clearly had plenty of flying experience.

As Sandra addressed herself to her plate, I wondered how she'd fit in. She was likeable enough. Then I reminded myself that I'd been in her position not that long ago. So much had happened since that fateful day when Jennifer and I had walked through the doors of Hawberry Hall.

"So how did you get to be the Boss?" Sandra asked me, popping the last morsel of toast into her mouth.

"She's the best woman for the job and she's proved it time and time again," said Maria, not mincing her words.

"Oh," was all Sandra said in response.

She must have sensed the change in atmosphere which immediately arose on her asking about my position. No more was said, and breakfast came to an end shortly afterwards. We all filed into the briefing room.

"She had better not start thinking she's going to try and take your place," said Maria in a low voice as Sandra went on ahead.

"I'm sure she won't," I replied. "We need to give her a chance." It was my job to integrate the newcomers as much as anything. I didn't want any more problems. It had been enough to contend with Linda in the past.

"I'll be keeping a close eye on her," said Maria ominously.

We sat down in our usual seats at the front of the room. I noticed that Sandra sat with the other new recruits. Perhaps Maria had scared her off a little. I resolved to try and be a little more friendly towards her. Though I too, was wary, simply on the grounds of experience. All of the new members would need to prove themselves, just as we had done.

James, Gloria and Henry entered the briefing room. We all immediately stood to attention as they took the podium.

"At ease," said James, which was the cue for us to be seated once more. "I'd like to start by welcoming once again the newest members of the Sirens."

There was a polite silence, during which he paused momentarily. I saw him glance at me and hoped he wasn't going to ask me to stand up and say something.

"For those who've just joined, you are now part of an elite unit — a strike force, and a deadly one at that. You are in the company of women who have proven themselves in combat and made a name for this squadron with those in the know in the RAF. You can be certain that all the most important people know about our exploits."

His gaze swept the room. I knew that this unit only existed because of his determination to show that women could handle combat just as well as the men. James would often speak passionately about the Sirens, in whom he had now invested his career, at least for the duration of the war.

"Once we feel you're ready, you too will fly combat missions over enemy territory. You will make a hugely valuable contribution to the war effort. I will remind you that everything we do here is top secret and can never be divulged. You've signed the Official Secrets Act, but the work of this squadron and indeed its very existence is only known to a select few. Certainly not to the Germans. We aim to keep it that way."

It was a stark reminder to us all. We relied on secrecy and stealth. Some of us had already gone to great lengths to protect it.

"All right," James said, "I'll hand over to Henry and Gloria, who will brief you on what comes next."

Henry stepped forward. "We're currently awaiting the delivery of six more Mosquitos," he said. "In the meantime, the new recruits will fly with experienced squadron members to learn the ropes, as well as getting the basic flight training and so forth. Navigators will attend classes separately for the purpose of learning how to navigate both day and night. Once that's done, you'll fly some training sorties. When you're mission-fit, you'll fly in combat."

He gestured to Gloria, who stepped forward.

"You'll be divided into two groups," she said. "Pilots in one group and navigators in the other. Pilots will be taken up with experienced pilots to speed up the process. When you are ready, navigators will fly on training missions. In addition, you'll be attending regular drill sessions, rifle and small arms training too. The schedule is posted on the noticeboard at the back of the room. If you need anything, ask. We are all here to help you integrate as quickly as possible."

"Thank you," said James. "You're all dismissed."

There was a hubbub of noise as the new recruits crowded around the noticeboard to check where they were meant to be. For the rest of us, now that we had completed our training and were on active service, our day-to-day life was less intense.

I was just about to leave the room when James appeared by my side.

"Anna," he said. "Might I have a word?"

"Of course, sir," I said.

He drew me aside, out of earshot of the others. I glanced at Maria and saw a smirk on her face, which I studiously ignored.

"I'm relying on you, Anna, to make sure the new recruits get up to speed."

"Absolutely."

"Thank you," he said formally, as there were eyes on us.

"All right, well, if that's all, sir?"

"Might I see you later?" he asked me tentatively.

"You might," I said with a smile.

"All right."

I saluted and he returned it before leaving. I already knew that Jennifer would be sleeping alone in our room that night.

CHAPTER FOUR

The days passed and we initially saw little of the new recruits. They were put through the same rigorous training regime we had completed. However, not long afterwards, I found myself sitting in the unfamiliar navigator's seat of my Mosquito, with Sandra in the pilot's seat, tasked with overseeing her first session in flight.

Sandra had loosely attached herself to our little group and often sat with us at mealtimes. Maria, in particular, was wary of her and I wondered if that was simply because Sandra was a little loud and outspoken. Regardless of any misgivings, I had to get her mission-fit, along with the other new recruits. Henry had put me in charge of the training session, and we needed to get started. I would be leading the flight from the navigator's position and calling the shots to the others over the radio.

"Well," said Sandra once we were strapped in, "I'm finally going to fly one of these things."

"Yes," I said. "We'll go up, do a few circuits, and then come back down. All right?"

"I think I can handle that," said Sandra, flashing me a smile.

"Fire it up then," I told her and waited while she started the engines. The two Merlin engines responded with a satisfying purr.

"Ooh, it sounds so … exhilarating," she said with great enthusiasm.

"Control, this is Gosling Leader, requesting clearance," I said over the radio.

"Roger, Gosling Leader, you're clear for take-off," came the response.

We'd taken the codename Gosling instead of our usual Bluebirds, to denote a training flight and differentiate it from the experienced flyers.

"Gosling Flight, check-in," I said and waited for all of the pilots to tell me they were ready to go.

"Roger," came the responses, one by one.

After this, I gave the order for the off. "Taxi to the end of the runway," I told Sandra.

"You got it, Boss."

Sandra opened the throttle and let off the brakes with the ease of an experienced pilot. There was a cutdown cockpit in the Hall where she and the others would have learned all the controls before being let loose on the real thing. However, it was clear that she was already an accomplished flyer.

The six Mosquitos taxied in a line to the end of the runway with us in the lead. Sandra braked, looked over to me and waited.

"Take her up," I told her.

A moment later we were hurtling along the runway, building up speed. I let Sandra decide when to get airborne, which she did with remarkable competence. So far so good.

"Let's do some circuits around the airfield," I said to her. "Get a feel for the plane."

"All righty."

She was smiling and I was pleased to see that she was in her element almost at once. The Mosquito was a lovely plane to fly, and she was taking to it like a duck to water.

"Gee, this is quite a beauty," she said. "Really nice to handle."

"Yes, it is," I agreed.

"What else can it do?" she asked after we'd done a few circuits.

"It can fly straight, hit the target and come home," I said in what I hoped were quelling tones. "That's our job."

"Oh." Her voice registered disappointment.

I hoped she wasn't thinking of trying anything clever with the plane. From her tone, it sounded as if that was her intention.

I tried to suppress the thought and said, "Goslings, let's fly away from the airfield and then come back. You can open up the throttle and see how that goes. Stay at this height."

I gave them a bearing while Sandra let the engines have their head. We picked up speed immediately and were soon barrelling along. The Mosquito was very fast and could outrun most fighters on the flat. It was interesting being in the passenger seat instead of flying. I was itching to take hold of the controls, but that was probably a natural reaction. Sandra wasn't making me nervous — in fact, quite the opposite.

"Yeeha," said Sandra. "That's more like it."

I watched the airspeed climb to around four hundred and told her to keep it steady. After a while, I gave the flight a bearing to take us back to the airfield.

"Can we go lower?" Sandra asked me on the return journey.

I was in two minds about this. It was our first time out, and low flying was an acquired skill. We'd done a lot of training for that particular purpose. However, on the whole, the new pilots seemed to be doing well, so there seemed no harm in dropping the height just a little.

"Goslings, you can take them down a bit, but not too low. I don't want any hedge-hopping, all right," I said, giving the order.

"Roger," came the response.

The next moment our Mosquito was heading towards the ground at an alarming rate.

"Sandra, what the hell are you doing?" I demanded.

"Just taking her down, Boss, like you said," replied Sandra, sounding not in the least concerned.

"Pull up, for God's sake."

To my annoyance, Sandra didn't respond immediately but kept going.

"One more second."

"Jesus Christ!" I exclaimed as she pulled up at the last moment, almost skimming the tall grasses in an open field. "When I said take her down, I didn't mean that bloody close to the ground."

"Sorry…"

However, Sandra sounded less than contrite and proceeded to fly us at breakneck speed towards a line of trees.

"Trees," I said. "Mind the bloody trees!"

"It's all right, Boss. I've seen them."

My heart was in my mouth as she pulled up and over at the last moment. I began to realise how things looked from Maria's perspective when I was flying this low. She continued at almost full throttle while the ground flashed by beneath us. We just managed to skim the rooftop of a house and then a barn. Gathering my wits, I decided enough was enough.

"Sandra," I said firmly, "I am ordering you to gain some height!"

"Okay, Boss, whatever you say," she said, gaining height once more.

I breathed a sigh of relief as the ground receded away from us.

"Goslings, return to base," I said, spotting the Tower in the distance.

"Roger."

"Is it over already?" Sandra asked me, sounding disappointed. "I was just starting to have fun."

"We're not here to have fun," I shot back. "We're here to learn to fly this Mosquito."

"Well, I did that pretty well, don't you think? I just wanted to show you what I'm capable of."

I didn't answer her because we had drifted lower again, either by accident or design. Right on cue, a series of telegraph lines loomed up ahead. I had a feeling of déjà vu as we hurtled towards them.

"For God's sake, Sandra!" I shouted, losing my cool. "I told you to gain height. What the hell are you doing?"

The lines were too close. I thought they were also probably too low to go under, the way I had done the other day. At the last moment, Sandra banked the plane sharply so that it ran parallel to the lines. This resulted in an immediate reproof from Jennifer in Gosling Two.

"Watch it, Gosling Leader, you almost hit us," she said.

Sandra had cut across her flight path, causing her to take evasive action. We continued to fly sideways until finally, Sandra banked away from the power lines. Then she righted the plane and levelled off. She glanced at me. I probably had a rather forbidding expression on my face at that moment.

"Just take us to the airfield and land it, if you please," I said quietly. "And that's an order."

"Yes, ma'am, right away," said Sandra, picking up on my icy tone.

Thankfully, she focused on the task at hand and took us down in an exemplary fashion. After executing a flawless landing, she taxied us back to our standing and cut the engines. I had to acknowledge she was a very competent pilot, but my blood was up.

Too angry to speak, I unstrapped myself, opened the hatch and jumped down without a word. Then I stood a little distance from the plane and waited for Sandra to appear while I tried to compose myself.

The others appeared at my elbow in short order.

"Anna, what were you...?" Jennifer began.

I pursed my lips and held up my hand for silence.

"Uh oh," said Patricia, eyeing me with some misgiving.

"Let's, erm, give the Boss some space," said Susan, motioning for the others to move back, which they did rather rapidly, but not out of earshot.

Sandra eventually emerged from the plane and walked over to where I was standing. She stopped in front of me.

"I realise that I possibly got a little carried away..." she began in a more conciliatory fashion, but she got no further.

"Carried away?" I cut in furiously. "You're lucky we weren't carried away in a bloody box! You not only endangered our lives, but the lives of two other crew members with your bloody stupid antics."

When I first became Flight Leader, I didn't know I had it in me to be quite so assertive, but leadership had changed me.

Sandra blenched at my unexpected onslaught. I had not finished, however.

"That was not only reckless, it was foolish beyond belief. You're in the Air Force now, not the circus. We are all responsible for each other's lives. What you did was bloody foolhardy, not to mention insubordinate."

"Yes, ma'am, I'm sorry, ma'am," said Sandra, finally finding her voice in the face of my tirade.

"So you should be," I told her. "If you want to be part of the Sirens, then you'd better start living up to the standards of this squadron."

"Ma'am," she replied.

I was about to say something further when I heard a voice behind me. It was Henry.

"I'll take it from here, Flight Leader," he said gently.

"All right..." I had run out of steam in any case. I saluted and withdrew.

"I won't repeat what FO Nightingale has already told you," I heard him saying to Sandra. "Suffice to say that was quite a performance, which we don't want to see again..."

I turned away and left them to it. Henry would no doubt be reading Sandra the riot act.

"What the hell was she doing?" asked Patricia as we climbed into the back of the truck.

"Showing me what a good pilot she is, apparently," I said.

"That went well then," said Jennifer sardonically. "It's a good job Nancy here has good reflexes."

SO Nancy Williams smiled at this. She was one of the new pilots, and had a fresh complexion and curly brown hair.

"I wasn't too fazed," she said. "I sort of saw it coming when Sandra was flying so close to the lines."

Patricia looked as if she was about to say something about my own exploits in that regard, but I shot her a warning look and she thought better of it.

"It's over and done," I said, wanting to put the incident behind us. "Let's hope it doesn't happen again."

"Whatever will James have to say about it?" said Susan.

I didn't know what he'd have to say, but I didn't have to wait long to find out.

Judy intercepted me not long after we'd arrived back at the Hall. We'd waited for Sandra, but since she hadn't appeared I'd asked the truck driver to drive on. Henry could bring her back, I'd decided.

"Wing Commander wants to see you, ma'am," said Judy.

I followed Judy to James's office. She let me in as usual and then shut the door behind me. James was seated at his desk, with Sandra standing in front of it.

"Ah, Anna," said James affably. "I was just having a talk with SO Brown about her recent flying lesson."

I walked up to the desk and saluted. Sandra turned to me and also snapped a salute.

"I'm sorry, ma'am," she said. "I was a bit impetuous, I know, and I apologise for my ill-judged behaviour."

"You can't do that in the Sirens," I told her. "We can't fly missions with someone who we can't trust to keep themselves in check."

She nodded and dropped her gaze. She reminded me of an errant schoolgirl who had been sent to the headmaster.

"I have explained to SO Brown that we have very exacting standards here. She needs to meet those standards if she is to continue flying with us," said James.

Sandra's eyes flashed suddenly at this. "I do understand, sir, I really do. I want to be in the Sirens," she said vehemently.

"Well, then I trust there won't be any repetition." James's tone was light but firm.

"No, sir, there won't."

He considered her for a moment before making up his mind. "All right, we'll say no more about it. Dismissed."

Sandra saluted us both and marched rather stiffly out of the room. Once she had gone and closed the door, James was at my side in a flash.

Nothing was said for a while as we kissed. The feelings this engendered never seemed to diminish; instead, they grew stronger and often left me breathless.

"I hear you were quite the tartar with her," he said, when he finally released me.

"I wouldn't say that," I replied, smiling. "I was rather cross."

"Not the way she told it."

He laughed and so did I. In a way, I was rather pleased to have made an impression on Sandra. Perhaps she wouldn't be quite so impetuous in future.

"What is she doing here, in the Sirens?" I asked him. "All the way from America."

"Ah," said James cryptically. "You'll have to ask our two friends from MI6 about that."

I frowned. It sounded like there was more to Sandra's presence than he was letting on. It also brought to mind the fact that the Marx Brothers had been unusually absent for a while.

"When are we going to see them again?"

"They'll be around soon enough," he said and quickly changed the subject. "How about lunch? Just you and me."

"I suppose you've already arranged it," I replied.

"I must admit, I took the liberty."

"You seem to be taking a lot of liberties recently," I teased, shooting him an arch look.

"Are you objecting?"

"Not entirely…"

As we made our way to the private dining room he sometimes used, I wondered if Sandra would keep her word. Something told me that she very possibly might not.

CHAPTER FIVE

There were thankfully no further incidents involving Sandra or any of the other new recruits, although I still harboured misgivings about her. For one thing, reports from other pilots flying with her intimated that she seemed to be just on the edge of pushing the boundaries. Not enough to remonstrate with her, but enough to give me concerns.

Other than that, training proceeded as normal and in the meantime, very few Operation Scorpion missions were flown. It seemed as if the operational emphasis had shifted for the time being. I wondered if there was something else in the offing.

As James had intimated, the Marx Brothers did eventually appear at Hawberry for a visit. I wondered if this presaged something new. In any case, I took the liberty of seeking an interview with them one morning.

I joined them in a room with high ceilings and wainscoting that they had previously used to question people, although this time I wasn't concealed in the hidey-hole which was accessed through a panel in the wainscoting. From there one could view the entire room and everything that went on in it. In the centre of the room itself was an ornately decorated table with a leather top. There was also a sofa and armchairs to one side. The Marx Brothers were seated in two of the armchairs when I entered.

They were dressed, as always, in dark suits with white shirts. One had a red tie and the other blue. I wondered if they had an endless supply of these, since the ties never seemed to vary. The two agents looked almost identical in appearance, with black hair and moustaches, apart from the fact that one had blue eyes and the other grey. They bore nicknames given to them by someone from another squadron. The two spies had revealed this to me at our first meeting and told me the person had no idea they knew about it, which they thought rather amusing. Harpo was the nickname of the man with grey eyes and Chico his colleague with blue eyes. I would probably never know their real names.

Their other distinguishing feature was their habit of smoking one cigarette after the other — an activity they were engaged in at that moment.

"Ah, Flight Officer," said Harpo, without getting up. Their manner was always informal.

"Hello," I said.

We were on friendly terms, and I rather liked them. They reminded me of characters in spy stories I had read when I was younger.

"And to what do we owe the pleasure?" said Chico, taking a drag on his cigarette.

I took a seat on the sofa. "I wanted to ask you about SO Sandra Brown," I said, getting straight to the point.

"Ah," said Harpo, in a tone that I took to be a bad sign.

Chico changed the subject at once. "How's the training going with the new recruits?" he asked.

"It's going quite well, apart from … well … Sandra," I replied, not willing to be deterred.

"Ah," said Chico, echoing his colleague.

"What do you both mean by … ah?" I demanded.

Chico took another long pull on his cigarette and then watched the smoke curl up towards the ceiling. "Well, you see, it's like this," he said at length and then paused.

Harpo picked up the thread. "It was, let's say, a favour for a favour."

I still didn't understand what they were talking about. "I'm not following you."

Harpo sighed. "Sandra left the USA under a bit of a cloud. We'd hoped not to have to reveal this, but there was bit of a … erm … scandal."

"What?" I interjected, flabbergasted at this disclosure. "What kind of scandal are we talking about?"

The two agents exchanged glances. After a moment, Harpo elected to speak.

"She had an affair with someone rather high up in the chain of command."

"Oh."

"And on top of that, she buzzed the President's party during a ceremonial flypast," Chico continued.

"Didn't go down well at all," said Harpo. "Spilt his drink over his suit and everything."

"The top brass was outraged," said Chico.

"So, you see —" Harpo started to say, but I cut him short.

"And you felt that bringing Sandra here to the Sirens was a good choice?" I said, somewhat acidly.

"Well, it wasn't so much a choice as a necessity," said Harpo.

In spite of myself, I was now intrigued. There was obviously more to it than they were letting on.

"Go on," I said.

Harpo resumed smoking and Chico took up the tale.

"Without going into too many details, in exchange for removing Sandra from the line of fire … certain favours were granted to us by the Americans. Things we needed: intelligence, other things…" He trailed off, since it was obvious he couldn't tell me what those other things were.

"So, you're telling me that Sandra was simply a transaction in some shady deal?"

"Not quite, but in essence … yes. Though I'd cavil at calling it shady," said Chico a little defensively. "Our allies are not always as forthcoming as we'd like, so…" He shrugged.

"And she is a damn good pilot," added Harpo.

"She may be a good pilot, but she's also potentially a loose cannon and she's supposed to fly combat missions, so how is that going to work?" I said a little heatedly.

Chico took another drag on his cigarette before speaking. "We were hoping that you'd be able to —"

He got no further because there was a knock at the door. I got up and opened it to find Maria.

"There you are, Anna, I've been looking everywhere for you. We've just had an urgent message from Control. It seems that Sandra has taken off in the Spitfire."

"She's done what?" I exclaimed.

"She's taken off … in the Spitfire," Maria repeated.

"Good God! All right, we need to get to the airfield pronto."

I flicked a glance at the Marx Brothers, who had not moved from their chairs. Harpo nodded as if he understood the urgency of the situation.

Maria and I rushed out to the trucks at the front of the building, where we were joined by Jennifer, Shelly, Connie and Patricia.

"We're coming too," they announced.

"Well, come on," I said. "There's no time to lose."

At my urging the truck driver made rapid progress and arrived at the airfield *tout de suite*. We jumped down from the truck and I spied Henry in conversation with one of the mechanics. We hurried over to him.

"You've heard, I take it," he said without preamble. "Sandra's taken the Spitfire."

"Yes, I've just been informed," I said.

"Control is trying to get her to come back."

"Never mind that," I replied. "Which way did she go?"

"You're not suggesting…?"

"Going after her? Yes, absolutely, we can outrun her for a start."

"You're hardly dressed for flying," said Henry.

"We'll take the chance."

He smiled and shrugged. He knew that when I had the bit between my teeth, there was no stopping me. Also, I felt responsible; Sandra was under my remit, after all. He didn't attempt to deter me.

"Go on then. See if you can persuade her to return and face the music."

"Let's just get her back here, first," I said grimly.

Maria and I climbed up into the Mosquito and strapped in. Our parachutes were kept in the planes, so that wasn't an issue. Although none of us had lifejackets on, I decided to chance it, as the likelihood of Sandra flying over water was slim.

I fired up the engines and we went rapidly through the preflight checks. The other two planes, with Patricia and Connie, plus Jennifer and Shelly, radioed in that they were ready to go.

"Control, this is Bluebird Leader requesting clearance," I said over the radio.

"Roger, Bluebird Leader, you're clear," said Control.

As I taxied to the end of the runway, Maria got a bearing from Control as to the approximate direction Sandra had flown in. There was no saying she'd stay on that course, but we had an advantage in that Jennifer's was one of the radar planes, and that would help us to spot the Spitfire.

"Bluebirds, let's go," I said, opening up the throttle.

The Mosquito pelted down the runway and we were soon airborne. The other planes settled on each of my wings. We turned as one onto the bearing Maria gave us.

"Keep a watch on the radar," I said.

"Wilco," said Jennifer.

"Just wait until I get hold of Sandra," said Maria to me as we gained height. She had been quietly simmering about the situation.

"I will deal with her, and so will James," I said firmly. "And in case you've forgotten, we took a B-17 without permission not long ago."

That had been quite an escapade, and even though we had a reasonable excuse, it still technically put us in the same boat as Sandra.

"Oh, fine, as you wish," Maria said with an exaggerated sigh.

I turned my attention back to the task at hand, which was to find Sandra. The sky was disappointingly empty, and I began to revise my hopes about her not going far. Her actions were foolish, since one couldn't be sure how much fuel the Spitfire had onboard, or ammunition for that matter.

Just as I was wondering how much further to go before turning back, the radio crackled to life.

"Radar contact," said Shelly triumphantly.

"Bearing?" said Maria at once.

I turned onto that bearing and after a few short moments, Maria shouted out, "There she is!"

Sure enough, the Spitfire in question was performing acrobatic loops, soaring through the sky like a bird, diving and swooping. No doubt Sandra was having the time of her life. I felt a pang of envy, as I had never flown a Spitfire. However, this wasn't the time for musing; it was my job to bring her home.

"Gosling One," I said, using her current codename. "This is your Flight Leader. Kindly return to base."

There was no response, so I tried again.

"Gosling One, are you receiving me? I need you to return to base."

The Spitfire levelled off abruptly.

"Oh, it's you," said Sandra.

"Yes, it's me, your Flight Leader and senior officer. I'm ordering you to return to Hawberry with us," I told her.

"I guess," she said. "If you say so…"

"I do say so!" I retorted, becoming a little frustrated.

Just as I was wondering how much longer Sandra was going to argue the toss with me, the situation escalated rather dramatically.

"Radar contact, heading our way," said Shelly suddenly.

"How many?" I asked her.

"Just one, but I don't know if it's a bandit or a friendly."

This was all we needed, I thought, with a sinking feeling in my stomach.

"Closing fast," continued Shelly.

"There it is," said Patricia urgently. "Bandit at two o'clock, heading straight for Gosling One."

I looked over and saw a Focke-Wulf Fw 190.

"Now we've got problems," said Maria. "Shouldn't we be getting out of here?"

"We can't leave Sandra to defend herself," I said, then over the radio, "Gosling One, you've picked up a bandit, take evasive action."

Sandra had seen the Wulf and instead of trying to get away, she was turning to engage with it. This was not what I wanted at all.

"For Christ's sake!" Maria was pardonably annoyed.

I thought fast. A deadly situation was rapidly developing. The advantage of distance was now lost, and Sandra couldn't outrun the Wulf in a Spitfire. Although the Mosquitos were not built for aerial combat, there were three of us against one — four, counting Sandra. That stacked the odds in our favour. I just prayed that she had some ammo.

"Bluebirds, break, let's go on the attack," I said.

Maria shot me a quizzical look. "What are you doing?" she asked.

"We've got no choice; plus, he's outnumbered."

The four of us started closing with the Wulf. The German didn't seem inclined to break off. Perhaps he optimistically thought he could shoot us all down. He kept on coming, while Sandra angled in from his side. She wasn't combat experienced and that worried me for a start. I knew from talking to James and Henry just how agile the Wulfs were in combat, and in the hands of an experienced pilot they were deadly.

Jennifer and Patricia had broken formation. They sensibly circled around in a pincer movement so that the Wulf would end up trapped between us. His best option was to turn and fly away, but he kept coming.

I could feel the adrenaline kick in as I realised we were in a life-or-death situation. A stream of tracers suddenly erupted from Sandra's Spitfire, but she wasn't close enough. The Wulf pilot flicked his plane aside, easily avoiding them. He turned and went on the attack. Sandra was also quick to bank away and pull a tight turn herself. She started to weave left and right, trying to evade him, while the Wulf settled on her tail.

We were almost in range, and I hoped one of us could get a shot in. I slipped the safety off the guns. I thought perhaps the Wulf was trying to shoot down the Spitfire, thinking we wouldn't engage him in the Mosquitos. He was wrong about that.

"He's on my tail. I can't shake him," said Sandra, sounding alarmed.

"Lead him to us, Gosling One," I said, the germ of an idea forming.

Perhaps if he was so intent on catching the Spitfire, the Jerry pilot wouldn't think about the fact he had trapped himself in the process. The Wulf fired a salvo, which Sandra only just evaded. I prayed she was going to be able to hold out as she turned her plane towards us, the Wulf in hot pursuit.

"When I say now," I told her, "I want you to go straight up, all right?"

"Roger, but make it soon, please…"

Both Maria and I heard the note of desperation in her voice. She had bitten off more than she could chew.

The Wulf fired again, and then a third time. In a way, this was good. He would be depleting his ammo. Sandra just managed to evade him, but then her luck ran out.

"I'm hit!" she said, after the Wulf took another shot. "I think he hit my wing."

I had to admire the way she was dealing with the situation, albeit that she had caused it in the first place. Then the moment came to act. Next time he fired, she might be dead. I wasn't having it.

"He's in range," said Patricia suddenly.

"I have him in range too," said Jennifer.

I glanced at my sights. It was likely that at least one of us could get him.

"You've got one chance," I told them. "So, take it —" I paused momentarily — "now!"

Right on cue, Sandra pulled up into a vertical climb at full throttle. The Wulf pilot was so intent on catching her that he followed suit. The manoeuvre exposed his underbelly, just as I had planned. I cut loose with the cannons at the same time as the other two Mosquitos. The Wulf didn't stand a chance. He flew into a hail of high-calibre bullets, which shredded his plane like balsa wood. The next moment, it exploded.

I banked away rapidly to avoid the flying debris.

"The bandit is down," said Jennifer triumphantly.

"We got him!" said Patricia.

"Any other radar signals?" I asked Shelly as I levelled off. I wanted to make sure there were no other bandits coming in behind the Wulf.

"Negative," she replied.

"Thank God for that," said Maria with some feeling.

Our luck was in, at least in that respect; it was time to get clear.

"Gosling One, form up with us; we're going home," I said.

"Roger," said Sandra without demur. I could hear the slight tremor in her voice.

"Give us the bearing," I said to Maria.

She did so and I turned the kite back towards Hawberry. The other two Mosquitos resumed their positions on my wings, and Sandra brought up the Spitfire to fly next to Jennifer.

"Thank goodness that's over," said Maria.

"Yes," I agreed, then got on the radio. "Control, we are returning to base with Gosling One. We were attacked by a bandit, which has been shot down."

"Roger, Bluebird Leader," said Control.

"What are you going to say to Sandra?" Maria asked me as we flew back.

"I don't know yet," I replied. She had endangered herself and all of us. However, I also remembered how I had flown against a Wulf on my very first flight in a Mosquito, when it had attacked Henry's Spitfire. Part of me admired Sandra's brazen approach to life. As Flight Leader, however, I couldn't allow her behaviour to go unchecked.

"I'm sure you'll work it out, Boss," said Maria with a smile.

I was glad she was ready to leave it to me. The last thing I needed was the other Sirens deciding to take matters into their own hands.

The airfield came into view but unfortunately, the surprises weren't over for the day.

"I've lost a lot of fuel," said Sandra. "The engine is cutting out."

"Keep going," I said. "Line up your approach first. Bluebirds pull back."

I eased the throttle on the Mosquito and the others did likewise. The Spitfire moved out in front and began to line up on the runway. I saw the propellor was still spinning, which was a good sign. My optimism, however, was short-lived.

"The engine's cut out," said Sandra.

"Take it easy, Gosling One," I said calmly. "You'll have to glide it in."

"All right, I'll try," Sandra replied.

The propellor of the Spitfire was now turning slowly as the kite lost power. I followed her as closely as I dared, hoping for the best.

"I ... I can't get the undercarriage down," said Sandra.

"Oh, come on! What else can go wrong?" said Maria in frustration.

Since none of us had flown a Spitfire, we had no idea how to help.

"Control, Gosling One can't lower the undercarriage and she's gliding in," I said.

"Roger ... there's a manual lever..." Control began.

The Spitfire was losing height fast. I could see Sandra would only just make it onto the runway.

"It's too late," said Sandra. "I'm going to have to land her on her belly."

"Roger, tenders are on their way," said Control.

We watched the Spitfire drop to earth with bated breath.

"It's all right, I think I'm going to make it ... yes ... oh my goodness..." said Sandra as the Spitfire ploughed onto the runway and started sliding down it at a crazy angle before finally coming to a stop. The canopy opened almost immediately and Sandra got out. She had the foresight to put some distance between herself and the plane as the fire tenders sped towards it. I doubted it would catch fire, but it paid to be safe.

I landed the Mosquito, pulled it up fairly short, then killed the engine.

"Come on," I said to Maria as she opened the hatch. "Let's go and see if she's all right."

We jumped down and made our way over to Sandra, who was still staring at the plane. The fire crews were checking it over. As we got closer, I could see her face was pale.

"She's in shock," I said to Maria in a low voice.

Sandra saw us approaching and turned away. Her shoulders began to shake and her hands came up to her face. Maria immediately ran to her and pulled her into a tight embrace. Maria was nothing if not compassionate. I stood back as James came running up, followed by Henry.

"Are you all right?" James asked me, looking concerned.

"Yes, but she's not," I said, indicating Sandra.

He glanced at Maria and Sandra, then smiled. "Well, at least you're all back down safely," he said.

"Not sure about the Spitfire," I replied.

"It's just a plane; it can be mended. A life can't be replaced," said James. "Come on, let's discuss this back at Hawberry. No sense in doing it out here."

I looked over to where Maria was still holding Sandra. She had clearly been quite affected by what had transpired. Maria gave me the thumbs-up. I signalled to the others to leave her to it, and we headed towards the trucks with Henry and James.

Sandra and I were seated at the meeting table in James's office, along with Henry, Gloria, Sandra and the Marx Brothers. I would have preferred less of an audience, but since they were involved one way or another, there was no help for it. Sandra was looking shamefaced, though seemingly much recovered.

"What possessed you to take the Spitfire without permission?" James asked Sandra now.

Sandra stared down at her hands, which were folded in her lap. "I just wanted to find out what it was like to fly. I'd heard so much about what a wonderful plane it was..." She trailed off.

"Where did you hear that?" asked James with interest.

"I'm not an ignorant woman," she retorted suddenly. "I talked with the other pilots when I was transporting planes. They said the Spitfire was a legend ... you know, from the Battle of Britain."

James smiled faintly. "Nobody is suggesting you're ignorant, or you wouldn't be here," he said.

"Sorry, I —" she began.

"Why didn't you just ask if you could fly it?" said Henry, cutting in.

"Because I didn't think you'd let me," she said candidly.

Both Henry and James laughed.

"None of the other Sirens have flown it yet," said James. "But then, none of them has asked either."

"Well then," said Sandra a little boldly, as if that endorsed her point. "Would you have let me?"

"I don't know," said James. "We've never thought about it. We've all been focused on the missions, getting the squadron fit to fly, that sort of thing."

"Point taken," she said, dropping her gaze.

"You put other Sirens in danger, SO Brown," James continued. "You could have been killed. As it was, one of the fuel lines on the Spitfire was cut by a bullet, which is why you lost fuel. You have created a lot of unnecessary repair work for the technicians... Shall I go on?"

Sandra shook her head. "I'm really sorry. It wasn't my intention to cause all this trouble."

"This isn't the place for kicking up a lark," put in Gloria. "It's serious business."

"No, ma'am," said Sandra. She sounded genuinely contrite. However, James wasn't finished.

"You've joined the Sirens with something of a reputation," said James, flicking a meaningful glance at the Marx Brothers.

Harpo and Chico said nothing but instead sat smoking their cigarettes, no doubt taking it all in.

"I suppose I have," said Sandra meekly.

"I was in two minds about taking you on," James continued.

Sandra fired up at once. "Kick me out if you must. Nobody wants me anyway."

I saw tears start in her eyes and reached out a hand to lightly touch her arm.

"Easy," I said to her. "Nobody is kicking you out."

"You might as well. Daddy didn't want me to join up; he said it wasn't seemly for women to serve in the forces. He was happy for me to fly for the Barnstormers, but not for my country. When I left to become a transport pilot, he told me not to come back..." She choked on a sob. "Even in the transport service some of the male pilots treated us like trash, putting sugar in our fuel tanks. Other women have died..." She burst into tears and put her hands up to her face. "I don't belong anywhere."

I moved closer and put my arm around her. She cried silently, and the others looked on. After a few moments, I produced a handkerchief from my pocket and handed it to her. She used it to dry her tears and blow her nose.

"I'm sorry," she said. "What must you think of me?"

"We think you're remarkably honest," said James. "And we admire that."

"And as for belonging," I said, "you belong here, with the Sirens, if you'll have us."

"If I'll have you?" she said incredulously. "I thought you wouldn't want me. Not after the trouble I've caused..."

"We're not all saints here, Sandra," I told her with a smile. "But we *are* a dedicated bunch of flyers."

"Who've already achieved some remarkable things," James put in.

"We're a sisterhood, and we'd like you to join, if you want to," I said.

Sandra suddenly got up from her chair and flung her arms around me.

I chuckled at her spontaneous display of affection. She let me go at length and sat back down.

"So, I can really stay?" she asked, wanting to make sure.

"If you promise not to take any more planes without permission," said James seriously.

"Oh, I promise," Sandra said earnestly.

"All right," said James. "But there are some consequences. You'll be stood down for two weeks, during which time you will report to Sergeant Wallace for drill every day, or whatever duties she sees fit to assign you."

"Every day?" repeated Sandra, her eyes wide.

"In addition, you will make a public apology to the entire squadron at the next briefing and pledge to follow orders in the future."

Sandra blenched a little at this, but I knew it was James's way. He had made Jennifer apologise in a similar fashion when she had disobeyed my orders during a practice flight.

"I expect to see exemplary behaviour from now on," he continued. "We look after our own here, but even we have limits."

James laid down the law in his inimitable way. He was firm but fair and quite forgiving where his charges were concerned. As much as possible he tried to keep any hint of a scandal internal, due to the detractors who were still out there with regards to the Sirens.

"I promise to behave, sir, and thank you for letting me stay," said Sandra.

"Then you're dismissed," said James.

Sandra stood up and saluted. She walked slowly from the room, as if she couldn't quite believe what had just transpired. When she had gone, the Marx Brothers spoke up.

"All's well that ends well," said Chico.

"Indeed," said Harpo.

"Let's hope so," agreed James.

"If there's nothing else, I'll go and see about my poor old Spitfire," said Henry.

James nodded, and the others took their leave. James and I were left alone.

"Well done, Anna," he said. "You handled things remarkably well."

"Remarkably? Didn't you think I could?" I said, unable to prevent a teasing tone creeping into my voice.

"Must you take me up on everything I say?" James said, laughing.

He came around to my side of the table and for a short while, I forgot about the war.

CHAPTER SIX

Sandra sat with us at breakfast the following morning. Following the Spitfire incident, Maria had taken Sandra under her wing. Sandra had no doubt told her what had transpired at the meeting with James.

"Drill's not so bad, once you get used to it," Shelly told her, tucking into her eggs on toast with beans. "We all had to do it for two weeks once…" She trailed off when she saw Maria's expression.

"Oh?" said Sandra, looking intrigued.

I sighed. There was no point in hiding anything if Sandra was going to be part of our group.

"I told you we weren't all saints," I said, cutting into the conversation. "Well, let's just say we borrowed a B-17 a while back…"

"Oh my God!" Sandra exclaimed, but she sounded impressed.

"It was for a good cause," said Pamela.

"And it's a long story," added Patricia.

"But I want to hear it. You can't just leave it there," Sandra protested.

"We'll tell you later," said Maria, glancing around the dining room. "When it's not quite so public."

"I'll look forward to that!" Sandra said, smiling.

The rest of us laughed. She didn't know the half of it. After breakfast, we assembled in the briefing room.

"There will be another mission tonight, as part of Operation Scorpion," said James from his usual place on the podium. He was accompanied by Henry, Gloria and the Marx Brothers.

"The mission leader will be Flight Officer Nightingale. She will be coordinating from the ground. All three crews flying the mission are posted on the noticeboard at the back. You can collect your mission orders from Flight Lieutenant Peterson."

I glanced at Sandra, who was sitting with us in the front row. She looked a little pale, anticipating what was coming next.

"An incident occurred yesterday," James continued. "I'm sure you're all aware of it by now. I'd like to invite SO Brown up here to say a few words about it."

Sandra stood up and made her way to the podium. James gestured for her to step forward. She hesitated for a moment, apparently gathering her thoughts.

"I'd like to say I'm sorry to everyone," she said, "and in particular to Wing Commander Donnington and Flight Leader FO Nightingale. What I did was incredibly foolish, and I hope that you will all forgive me."

She paused and glanced around at the sea of faces.

"I know that some of you think I'm a loud Yank who thinks a lot of herself —" there was a ripple of laughter at this — "but I want nothing more than to be part of the Sirens, and to prove myself in combat. I want to show you that I'm worthy of being your colleague, and I hope you'll accept my apology."

"Three cheers for Sandra!" shouted Maria, suddenly getting to her feet. "Hip hip hooray!"

I saw Sandra's eyes glisten as the cheers echoed around the room.

"All right, thank you, SO Brown. Very well said; you may step down," said James when a hush had fallen once more.

Sandra returned to her seat next to Maria, who took her hand and squeezed it.

"All right, now that's out of the way, you can all go about your duties. Dismissed," said James. He left the platform, but not before our eyes met briefly. I smiled to myself and wondered how long we could keep our relationship under wraps.

"You're one of us now," Maria was saying to Sandra, who seemed a little overwhelmed by her reception.

"Well done, Sandra," I said to her.

"Thank you, Boss," she said, smiling. "And thank you for putting up with me."

"You're more than welcome," I replied. It was time to let bygones be bygones. There was a war to fight, after all.

Our little band assembled in my and Jennifer's room after we'd finished our duties. It had become our informal HQ. Shelly produced a bottle of rum and passed it around.

"Where did you get that? Are we allowed it?" Sandra asked in surprise.

"She's got contacts," said Susan.

"What she means is, Shelly has multiple boyfriends from whom she garners favours like alcohol," said Maria, by way of explanation.

"Now, that's not fair," said Shelly. "I only have one boyfriend at a time."

Maria rolled her eyes and the rest of us laughed. I looked over to where Jennifer and Connie were sitting by the open window. They were sharing a cigarette and talking in low voices.

Jennifer smiled at me, and I suppressed the rising fear I always got when she flew a mission without me. I didn't know how I would cope if I were to lose her.

"Go easy on the rum, Shelly," I said. "I want you sober on that radar tonight."

"Oops, sorry, Boss," Shelly replied, looking contrite.

SO Judith Ellington and ASO Cynthia Jones were flying the same mission, along with SO Molly Chingford and ASO Eileen Rutherford as the third crew. Molly and Eileen had replaced SO Ruth Maddison and ASO Brenda Biggins, who were killed on the Carlingue raid.

Patricia and Maria regaled Sandra with the story of our B-17 escapade while her eyes grew wider and wider.

"Wow," she said. "You girls have beaten any high jinks I ever got up to."

"We're not planning a repeat performance," I said sternly.

"But if you do," said Sandra with great enthusiasm, "count me in."

"You're a game bird, I'll give you that," said Patricia, laughing.

The minutes crawled by, but soon enough it was time to go. I left Jennifer and Connie alone in the room to say goodbye and went downstairs to wait. As much as any of us believed we would come back, we never knew for sure. Things could go very wrong very fast on a mission.

"Are you coming with us?" Jennifer looked surprised when she found me by the truck, along with Maria. It was quite a balmy night, not too dark and good for flying.

"I'm going to see you off," I said. I didn't add that it was because I might never see her again, though I was sure she knew.

"And where the Boss goes, I go," said Maria.

"All right then, well, let's get going," Jennifer replied, climbing into the back of the truck. She and Connie sat together, sharing a cigarette as we wound our way down to the airfield. It was understandable that Connie would also want to say goodbye.

Leading Aircraftwoman Victoria Singleton was waiting by the aircraft in her usual mechanics' overalls.

"All ready, fully fuelled and loaded, ma'am," she informed me, snapping a salute.

"Thank you," I said.

Victoria had become a confidante following an investigation into the sabotaging of our planes. As a result, she always made sure she personally oversaw the preparation of the planes for our missions.

"Well," said Jennifer, "better get on with it, I suppose."

I flung my arms around her and held her tight. "Come back safe, my darling," I whispered.

"Don't worry about me," Jennifer replied with her usual insouciance.

She and the others walked to the planes. Connie went with her, and they stole a surreptitious kiss under the wing of Jennifer's Mosquito.

"She'll be all right," said Maria. "I'm sure of it."

"I hope so," I said, unable to prevent the sinking feeling in my stomach.

We watched the Mosquitos fire up their engines, and then rumble down to the end of the runway. In short order, they took off and disappeared into the night.

"I don't suppose you're going to sleep tonight, are you?" Maria remarked with some perspicacity, as we climbed back into the truck.

"I can try," I said, but it would difficult when I knew Jennifer was flying into danger.

"I'll keep you company if you want?" said Maria, noting my hesitation.

"All right."

True to her word, she sat with me into the small hours. We talked of this and that until eventually, my eyes began to close. I lay down fully clothed and drifted off to sleep. My dreams were filled with visions of Jennifer's plane getting shot down. I woke with a start and in the silence, I heard the sound of a truck returning.

I sat bolt upright to see Maria sleeping in the single bed next to mine. She woke at once.

"Are you all right?" she said, sitting up too.

"I heard the truck…" I said, trying to shake the nightmare from my sleepy brain.

"Come on," said Maria. "Let's go and meet them."

We hurried down the stairs and into the atrium at the main entrance, which was beginning to show the first signs of predawn light. Four people entered: Judith, Cynthia, Molly and Eileen. Jennifer and Shelly were not there.

I scanned their faces. They were looking grave.

"Where's Jenny?" I demanded at once.

The others hesitated, but then Cynthia, the Scottish navigator, spoke up.

"Her plane was hit, Boss. They went down…" She trailed off.

"Went down where?" I asked, trying to take it in.

"Over the Channel; we're not sure, to be honest. It all happened so fast," she replied.

"What happened?"

"We took some flak, got chased by a couple of bandits. We managed to outrun them, but Jenny's plane was hit. She managed to make it to the Channel and ordered us to fly on. We didna' want to, but those were her orders…"

I stared at them in shock.

"What was their last position?" asked Maria. "We need that."

Cynthia gave it to her. I felt numb, unable to speak. Jennifer was gone. My sister was gone. We stood there like a frozen tableau, and then suddenly James was at my side.

"What's happened?" he asked.

I turned to him, holding back the tears. "Jennifer ... she ... she's..."

"Her plane went down," said Maria, "in the Channel. We don't know any more than that."

James took charge at once. "You lot better get yourselves something to eat. We can debrief later," he said to the others. "Anna, Maria, come with me. We will work out what to do."

"I've got the last bearing," said Maria.

"That's good," said James. "It will help us look for her."

We turned to go, only to see Connie, who had arrived silently and was staring at us.

"Where's Jenny?" she said.

"She went down over the Channel," said Maria.

"No, not Jenny! Not my Jenny!" Connie cried out in anguish. Her body started to crumple. Maria caught her just in time.

"I'll take care of her," she said. "You go on."

James took my arm and gently guided me up the stairs to his quarters. Once there, he sat me down on the sofa, went over to the sideboard and poured out a glass of whisky. He came back to me and set it down.

"Drink this," he said.

"I don't want it," I murmured.

"Drink it, please. It will help."

I picked it up and downed it in one go. The liquid burned my throat, but it was somehow warming too.

"Now, listen to me," he said. "Before you go thinking your sister is dead, we don't know that. At first light, we'll get the squadron out to look for her."

"I had a nightmare," I told him, still in a daze. "I dreamt Jenny was shot down, and now it's come true."

"Stop it," he said. "We're going to find her. I promise you that."

I dissolved into tears. This was too much to bear. I was in James's arms in an instant. He held me close and stroked my hair. Somehow it helped.

CHAPTER SEVEN

I woke up in James's bed. He was standing by his dresser, putting the finishing touches to his uniform. He turned to me and smiled.

"How are you feeling?"

"Afraid," I told him, truthfully.

"Well, I suggest you go back to your room and put on your flying gear. After breakfast we'll call a briefing and get a search organised, all right?" His tone was matter-of-fact, but sympathetic. He'd been everything I needed a few hours earlier. I had not realised until then how much I *did* need him. Perhaps it took a tragedy to do that.

I had wanted to go sooner to look for Jennifer and Shelly, but James wouldn't hear of it. If they were okay, then they'd be in a dinghy, floating somewhere in the Channel. If they weren't, then it was already too late. Besides, they might get picked up by a passing Navy ship.

Breakfast was subdued. Connie looked heavy-eyed and tearful. I immediately missed Shelly's sunny disposition and the banter that went with it. I forced down my eggs, toast and beans along with a cup of tea. Eventually, Maria had had enough of the sombre atmosphere.

"Listen, you lot," she said, "Jenny and Shelly aren't dead, as far as we know, so for God's sake let's all cheer up."

I gave her a weak smile. "Maria's right," I agreed. "We need to stay positive."

I was a little at odds with my emotions. After all, bomber crews flew out daily and didn't come back. People were killed in action all the time. That didn't stop the prospect of it hurting. What would I tell my parents? I felt Maria's hand slip into mine as if she understood.

Shortly afterwards, the squadron assembled in the briefing room. James, Henry, Gloria and the Marx Brothers were standing on the podium, looking serious. The Marx Brothers weren't even smoking for a change.

"All right," said James, when the room was called to order. "I'm sure you know that SO Nightingale and ASO Cartwright's plane went down in the Channel last night while returning from a mission — which was successful, by the way. The squadron will fly a search pattern over the last position before the Mosquito went down. Flight Lieutenant Peterson will brief you. The search will be led by FO Nightingale. We will coordinate things from this end by radio."

He paused to allow us to absorb this.

"We haven't received any word from coastal command about downed aircraft, but if we do, we'll radio it through. We all know that it's a fact of war that things like this happen. It doesn't make it any less of a tragedy, at least for this squadron."

There was silence at his words. The loss of any member of the Sirens would be keenly felt. The loss of a sister.

"That being said," James continued, "I prefer to look on the optimistic side and believe that they are out there somewhere and that we'll find them."

Henry took over and explained how the search would work. We'd fly to the starting point, fan out in a line, then fly up and down the Channel trying to cover as much ground as we could. There was a lot of water to cover, and we couldn't go too close to France for obvious reasons. It helped that the ditch point was nearer to the English coast, however.

Shortly afterwards, we headed for the planes. Connie sat in the back of the truck, smoking. It was strange not to see Jennifer sharing a cigarette with her.

As I jumped down from the truck, I was met by Victoria.

"I hope you find them, ma'am," she said.

"I hope so too."

With that, we boarded our planes and strapped in. I fired up the engines. I looked at Maria and she looked at me.

"We are going to find them," she said fiercely.

I nodded. "Yes."

The entire squadron had been pressed into service, including the new pilots and navigators. They were all now part of the Bluebird callsign, even though some of them had not yet completed their training. It just made more sense to keep it that way. Two callsigns on one flight would be confusing.

"Control, this is Bluebird Leader requesting clearance," I said to the Tower.

"Roger, Bluebird Leader, you're clear to go."

"Bluebirds, let's get this show on the road," I said, letting off the brakes and taking the Mosquito down to the end of the runway.

It was good to be doing something constructive, and all the training immediately kicked in. I throttled up the kite and we headed down the runway at high speed. Moments later we were airborne. I circled the airfield, waiting for the rest of the flight, then called them to order.

"Bluebirds, close formation, follow my lead," I said.

Maria gave them the bearing and I turned towards the South Coast, keeping a decent height. There was no need for low-level flying. Jennifer's plane had apparently started to go down a few miles south of Worthing, so that would be the place to begin. Since the Mosquito was made of wood, there was a chance it might float for some time, although it also had two heavy engines and plenty of other things to weigh it down.

We reached the waypoint where the last contact was made. I gave the order to begin the search. It was a sunny, cloudless day. The water was calm, which helped.

"Bluebirds, wide formation, on me. Keep your eyes peeled for bandits," I said.

I turned the flight due east. There was always the possibility of enemy contact. The Germans would have clocked us on their radar for sure. They might send out a squadron to see what we were doing. I hoped not. I had discussed this with James and my orders were to break off and head for the English coast. He would get Fighter Command to scramble a defence.

We flew as far as Hastings, turned back and flew the other way without incident. We only had one radar plane now, and it was vital as a lookout in case of enemy incursion.

"Nothing so far," said Maria as we passed the Isle of Wight, turned back again and moved closer to the English coastline.

"Radar contact," said Pamela suddenly.

I sighed. This was all we needed.

"How many and how far?" I asked her.

"Looks like three and some distance away," she responded.

"Over there, on our three o'clock," said Maria, pointing.

Sure enough, three Focke-Wulfs could be seen in the distance, flying parallel with us.

"What shall we do, Boss?" asked Patricia.

"Stay on course, unless they do something," I told her. I was reluctant to cut and run just then. Perhaps they were just checking up on what we were doing. I radioed Control.

"Control, we've three bandits tracking our course but currently not engaging," I said.

"Roger, Bluebird Leader, we're scrambling a squadron to see them off," said Control.

I continued our flight up to Hastings once more, turned back and moved closer to the coastline yet again. The Wulfs stayed with us. Minutes ticked by and I kept flicking anxious glances at the enemy planes, but they did not seem inclined to get any closer.

"Here comes the cavalry at last," said Maria.

A squadron of Spitfires roared overhead in the direction of the Wulfs. They dipped their wings as they passed.

"Did you see that?" asked Maria.

"See what?" I asked. I hadn't really taken much notice of the planes.

"The badges on those planes — the 'Spitfire Mavericks'. Strange name, don't you think?"

It *was* odd, I thought, but then we had a nickname too — the Sirens. Doubtless other squadrons did the same.

"Well, perhaps they're a bit like us. We're mavericks too," I said.

"You mean they're women?" Maria said in surprise.

"No," I laughed. "I mean, perhaps they're just different to the run-of-the-mill pilots."

"We'll never know, anyway," said Maria.

That much was true. We wouldn't have contact with any other squadrons due to our top-secret nature. That was the luck of the draw.

We watched the Spitfires close with the Focke-Wulfs, who swiftly thought better of hanging around and headed for France. The Spitfires continued to fly after them until the German planes had almost disappeared. Then the Mavericks squadron turned back to Blighty and passed over us once again. We had to maintain radio silence, so we weren't allowed to talk to the other squadrons. Besides which, we had a special frequency. One of the pilots gave us a wave, and Maria waved back.

With the immediate problem over, I turned my attention to the sea, which was disappointingly empty. At the Isle of Wight, we turned back and flew closer still to the coast. I was beginning to lose hope as we passed the Seven Sisters cliffs. But then, just as we rounded the corner at Beachy Head, the radio crackled to life.

"There it is, a Mosquito, down there," said Sandra, who was closer to the shoreline than we were.

Sure enough, there was Jennifer's plane. It appeared to have drifted almost into the cliffside.

"Oh God, it's them, it's really them," said Maria.

Except it wasn't. There was no sign of life on the plane.

"Control, Bluebird Four has been spotted, down by Beachy Head," I told them.

"Roger, Bluebird Leader, anyone in it?" came the response.

"Negative."

My heart sank, but I told myself that this was no time to lose hope.

"Go down for a closer look, Bluebird Leader," said Control.

"Wilco." I gave the order to the others. "Bluebirds, circle around while I check out the plane."

"Roger," came the response from each of the others in the flight.

I dropped the Mosquito to almost wave height and flew a pass over the plane. The overhead hatch was open, which was probably a good sign. It meant they had probably escaped. But if so, where were they?

"Did you see anyone in it?" I asked Maria.

"No, but go again, just to make sure," she said.

"All right."

I circled around and flew over it again, going as low as I could. The cockpit was definitely empty. There also seemed to be a rather large gash in one wing. Dreadfully disappointed, I gained height and rejoined the squadron.

"Control, there's nobody in the plane," I said.

"Roger, standby."

We continued to circle, waiting for orders.

"What happens now?" said Maria.

"I don't know," I said. "We can keep searching, I suppose…" I trailed off. We both knew that if they had been in the water, we'd have seen them by now.

"Bluebird Leader," said Control. "Wing Commander's orders are to destroy the plane."

"Say again, over," I said, not quite able to believe it.

"Orders are to destroy the plane and then return to base."

Maria and I looked at each other. There was nothing for it. The Sirens couldn't leave any evidence behind. There was the radar, and there might be mission orders in the plane too. It had to be done.

"Wilco," I said and then, "Bluebird Two and Bluebird Six, form up on me. We will strafe the Mosquito and then do a bombing run, in sequence."

"Roger," said Patricia.

"Roger," said Susan.

"All right," I said to Maria. "Let's do it."

I flew out a little distance from the cliffs, with Susan and Patricia on my wings. Then I dropped down, skimming low over the water. I throttled up and headed for the ditched plane, easing off the safety.

When we were in range, I gave the order.

"Fire," I said as I opened up with the cannons. The bullets from three planes ripped up the water and hit the Mosquito. It started to catch fire. We passed over it and I pulled a tight turn to come back for a bombing run. The ordnance was always loaded, just in case.

"I'll take first crack," I said. "Bluebird Two, you will follow, and then Bluebird Six."

"Roger," came the response.

I opened up the bomb bay doors as we flew towards the plane. Bombing runs had become routine and although the Mosquito was burning, it wasn't destroyed.

"Now," said Maria.

"Bombs away," I said.

The bombs flew towards the target and as we got clear, they exploded. The fuses were always set, giving us time to get clear. Patricia followed me in for another run, and then Susan. Once the dust had settled, I flew around for another look. There was very little left of the plane. One bombload would probably have been enough, but it was better to be on the safe side.

"Control, target destroyed," I said flatly.

"Roger."

It was over and done. Jennifer and Shelly hadn't been found, just an empty plane.

"Control, we're returning to base," I said, gaining height. "Bluebirds, close formation, let's go home."

The return to Hawberry was filled with mixed emotions. I knew that once we landed, the loss of Jennifer would hit me. I was determined to try and keep my composure, at least in public. I tried to put it to the back of my mind and focus on flying the plane. Maria didn't talk, but she kept stealing worried glances in my direction. The reality of war had hit home in the most horrific way possible with the loss of my sister.

The airfield came into view, and I started to line up for a landing.

"Control, permission to land," I said over the radio.

"Permission granted," said Control.

"Here we go," I said to Maria, taking the kite down just as I had dozens of times before. The wheels touched the ground and I taxied the Mosquito to the standing with a heavy heart. As I killed the engine, I struggled to hold back the tears.

Maria's hand touched my arm suddenly. "Save it," she said quietly.

"What?" I asked, my voice raw with emotion.

"Look over there…"

I turned in the direction she was pointing. Leaning against a jeep were Jennifer and Shelly, large as life.

"Oh my God!" I screamed. "Open the door, open the bloody door!"

"I'm doing it, I'm doing it," said Maria, laughing.

She dropped the hatch and jumped down. I followed suit and the next moment I was pelting over to Jennifer at top speed.

"Anna!" she called out as I got closer, but I didn't stop. I flung myself into her arms.

"You're safe, you're safe! I thought you were dead," I said, sobbing into her shoulder.

"Of course I'm not dead, Anna," said Jennifer prosaically.

"Oh, Jenny," I said crossly, pulling out of her embrace. "Where have you been? Why didn't you get in contact?"

"It's a long story," said Jennifer.

Just then, her attention was claimed by Connie. Jennifer took her into her arms and Connie burst into tears. I turned to Shelly and hugged her too, for good measure.

"I'm glad you're back," I told her.

"Did you miss me?" she asked, laughing.

"Like we miss the devil," replied Maria, in a voice loaded with affection.

We were joined by the rest of the squadron, and the next moment we were all hugging, patting each other on the back and laughing.

"Gosh," said Jennifer. "We've only been gone a few hours."

"Too many hours for me," said Connie.

"I'm sorry." Jennifer's voice softened at once. "We couldn't get in touch, otherwise we would have."

"SO Nightingale, ASO Cartwright, I'm very glad to have you back."

It was James, who had arrived unnoticed.

"We're very glad to be back, sir," said Jennifer, snapping a salute out of habit.

"Never mind all that. Come on, let's return to base," said James. "Then you can tell us all about it."

"Yes, sir," said Jennifer.

We jumped into the waiting trucks and headed back to Hawberry. Once there, we all assembled in the briefing room.

"SO Nightingale, ASO Cartwright," said James. "You have the stage."

Jennifer and Shelly stood up on the podium and began to speak. Behind them stood James, Henry, Gloria and the Marx Brothers.

"Well," Jennifer began, "this isn't at all how we expected things to turn out."

There was a ripple of laughter. It lightened the mood.

"The mission went exceedingly well. We strafed the target, dropped the bombs and then the ack-ack opened up."

"Things got pretty hairy," Shelly added. "Particularly when a piece of flak took a chunk out of our wing."

There was an audible gasp at this. Jennifer continued.

"We carried on regardless — the Mosquitos seem to be able to take some damage — but then we picked up a bandit. Of course, we tried to outrun him, but we were just a little slower because of the wing. He chased us over the Channel ... took some potshots at us. He hit us, I think, because one engine caught fire. I told the others to go on ahead and decided to ditch — it was the only thing to do..."

She trailed off and turned to look at James. He nodded in approval.

"Fortunately, the bandit broke off contact as we dropped towards the sea. The water was pretty calm and so I managed to land it all right. Luck was on our side. Then, we got into the dinghy and rowed to shore. Turns out we weren't that far from Blighty after all."

Another burst of laughter eased the tension.

"We found a barn and went to sleep in the hay," said Shelly, taking up the tale. "The farmer found us this morning and offered us breakfast, thank goodness, because I was bloody starving! Anyway, we wanted to get in touch, but the farmer didn't have a telephone. So, we cadged a few lifts..."

"And here we are," said Jennifer, finishing the sentence for her.

"Thank goodness for that," said Patricia loudly and everyone laughed.

"You both did admirably," said James, stepping forward. "Exactly what I'd expect from the Sirens. I'm glad you made it back."

"I'm sorry we lost our plane," said Jennifer. She would know by now that it had been destroyed, along with the radar equipment.

"Planes can be replaced," said James, echoing his earlier sentiments. "You can both step down; thank you for the debrief. Most enlightening."

Jennifer and Shelly returned to their seats and James continued.

"I think this is a lesson for everyone," he said. "Be vigilant, and watch out for flak, obviously. If you have to ditch, do your best to get out of enemy territory first."

We all knew that if we were shot down or forced to ditch in enemy-occupied territory, we would be expected to destroy the aircraft. That was the reason we carried grenades on missions.

"This could also signal that the Germans are becoming more vigilant. After all, we've been attacking their airbases recently; they're probably getting fed up with it. Speed is key. Get in and get out as quickly as possible. In case you're wondering, these missions will continue for the time being."

It was to be expected. We had a duty to carry out and we would do it no matter what.

"I think that's enough for today," said James. "Lunch is in order. Duties are cancelled for the afternoon. Everyone deserves a well-earned break, especially SO Nightingale and ASO Cartwright."

"Woohoo!" said Shelly, making everyone laugh once more.

"Dismissed," said James with a smile.

Now that the Sirens were once more complete, we made our way to the dining room in a buoyant mood.

That night I lay in James's arms. I was spending more time with him in spite of myself. Most nights I would go to his room and then creep back to my own in the early hours. I'd find Jennifer asleep in our double bed and she would cuddle up to me, but no word was said about James.

"I'm going to have to ask you to go out on another mission," James said quietly.

"Well, it's my job," I replied.

"I can't help wishing it wasn't."

"Oh?" I turned to him. "Why not?"

He sighed. "Don't get me wrong, you're a fantastic pilot," he said in earnest tones.

"Then what?"

He paused, looking directly at me. "I don't want you to die," he said at length.

Having a combat role in the war meant that I and the rest of the Sirens risked our lives every day, even if no one knew it. It was just a fact of life for us as a top-secret squadron. However, the very real possibility of death was not something James and I had discussed before, and I took it as an indication of his depth of feeling for me.

"I don't want to die either, and I don't intend to if I can help it," I said.

He didn't answer, so I elected to cajole him a little.

"Just remember, you started this women in combat thing," I teased.

"Don't I know it," he said.

"And what is that supposed to mean?"

"It means that I'm very glad I did," he said.

"That is the right answer, Wing Commander," I told him. "And as you well know, it's my duty as Flight Leader to set a good example."

"Is that what you're doing now?" he murmured, reaching for me.

"I'm off duty now, so…" I didn't finish the sentence and instead surrendered to his lips once more.

CHAPTER EIGHT

The mission came around all too soon. It was another three-plane sortie against a German airbase in France. I was naturally named as mission leader, along with Susan in the only radar plane, and Sandra.

James had consulted me about the mission crew. I'd selected Sandra without hesitation.

"It's time to see if she can handle it," I said. James had already told me that the new recruits were combat-ready.

"All right, you're the Boss, but don't let her do anything stupid."

We laughed at his use of my nickname.

Maria was a little more forthright when expressing her opinion of my choices.

"You're bringing Sandra on the mission? Have you taken leave of your senses?" she demanded.

"No," I said. "I think she'll do just fine."

"You know I want to come back from this alive, don't you?" she said.

"So you tell me *every* time," I said with an exaggerated sigh. "Look, if I didn't think she was up to it, I wouldn't take her."

"Fine, fine, whatever you say." Maria waved her hand dismissively.

It was a dark night as Maria and I climbed into the truck to join Susan, Pamela, Sandra and ASO Lucy Morgan, one of the new navigators Sandra had teamed up with. I had said goodbye to James in private.

"Come back safely," he'd told me.

"I'll do my best," I'd replied.

I knew from bitter experience that it was worse for the person left behind than the one going on the mission. My thoughts returned to the task ahead.

"Here we go again," said Pamela as the truck set off towards the airfield.

"First time for me," said Sandra.

"Just stick with us and you'll be fine," Maria told her.

Sandra flashed her a smile. She had been trying to stay in everyone's good books since the Spitfire incident.

I had briefed everyone thoroughly. The mission was part of Operation Scorpion. We would head down to Folkestone, cross the Channel and make landfall just west of Calais. Then we'd turn east, hit the target — an airfield near Calais — and return to Hawberry. It ought to be a straightforward mission. But experience had taught me nothing was ever straightforward in war.

The truck came to a stop and we jumped down from the back.

"All right, Sirens," I said. "Let's get to it."

"Yes, Boss," they all replied in unison.

We walked over to our waiting Mosquitos. I had a brief word with Victoria, who assured me all was right and tight. Then Maria and I climbed up into the cockpit, closed the hatch and strapped in.

"Ready?" I asked her.

"As I'll ever be," she said with a smile.

I fired up the engines and waited for the others to check in. Once they had done so, I radioed the Tower.

"Control, this is Raven Leader requesting permission to take off," I said.

"Raven Leader, you're clear to go."

"Roger."

"Ravens, let's do this," I said to the others. Ravens was the codename we'd picked for our callsigns.

I steered the Mosquito out from the standing and headed for the end of the runway, followed by the others. Once there, I pulled to a stop and began to wind up the engines for take-off. I let off the brakes and we barrelled down the runway. Moments later we were airborne. The others followed and joined us shortly afterwards.

"Ravens form up, close formation, low level," I said.

They closed in on my wings, Maria gave out the bearing and I steered us onto the heading. The route took us cross country, east of London. I dropped the Mosquito down to treetop height and opened up the throttle. The ground flashed by beneath us at a tremendous pace as my eyes quickly adjusted to the dark landscape. I flicked a glance at the other two planes, particularly Sandra's, but she seemed to be keeping up. Her training had been thorough.

I turned my focus on what was in front of us, while Maria called out the hazards.

"Lines," she said, as some telegraph poles came into view.

"Got it," I replied, making sure I passed over them and not under them this time.

"House."

"Yep."

"Trees."

"Seen them."

We passed Saffron Walden, Bishop's Stortford and then Chelmsford — all darkened towns with hardly a light showing due to the blackout. I wondered how they must have looked at night from the air before the war, with streetlamps aglow and lights shining from houses. People without a worry, other than what the neighbours might be doing. Now they lived in constant fear of being bombed by Jerry.

"Thames coming up," said Maria as we passed Basildon and headed for Gravesend.

The tide was in as we flew low over the inky black water and the black hulks of ships and barges anchored or moving slowly upriver. We passed by Sittingbourne, then turned towards Ashford and the coast at Hythe. In a few moments we crossed the whiteness of the beach and then we were over the Channel. I shivered slightly as I thought of Jennifer, ditching in the black water. The moon left a shimmering trail over the waves as we skimmed as low as we could.

"Ravens, kill the lights," I said, flicking off the navigation lights.

We were now effectively in enemy territory and reliant on the radar to detect any enemy planes in the darkness. I hoped we wouldn't encounter any.

It was a straight run to a town called Wissant, where we would make landfall. It was a less heavily defended route into France. The idea was to cut east behind Calais and then to the airfield, which lay at Calais-Marck. It was one of the more frequently attacked airfields by the RAF, apparently, meaning it was well used by the Luftwaffe.

We maintained radio silence to avoid letting the Germans zero in on us. There was nothing to break the silence bar the hum of the engines as we flew over the water. Then, all too quickly, the French coastline was in sight.

We flew over the beach and then we were over countryside. Fields flashed by — a patchwork blanket of light and dark in the monochrome landscape. A few moments later, Maria gave us a new bearing. We stayed low, hopping up and over hedges, houses, treelines. Our conversation consisted of one-liners as the tension mounted. It was always like this on a mission. Anticipating what was to come, plus the constant fear of discovery.

The route took us across the least populated areas, avoiding towns and villages and keeping low all the way to avoid radar detection by the Germans.

"Chip shop in five," Maria said, giving out a new bearing. Chip shop was the codename for the target. We changed them every mission to confuse the enemy who listened in on transmissions.

"Roger," I said, turning due north.

This was it. The airfield was just up ahead. My heart began to race as the adrenaline coursed through my veins. I slipped off the safety on the guns. We sped towards the town of Marck, keeping low. Just beyond it was the airfield. I was about to call 'attack formation' when Pamela's voice cut in.

"Radar contact, dead ahead."

My heart sank. This wasn't what we needed.

"How many?" I asked her.

"Two, possibly three, heading for an intercept."

I thought fast. Could we still make it to the airfield and drop the bombs? It might be possible under the cover of darkness, if we were lucky. Then our luck ran out as the airfield searchlights came on. The beams probed the sky, searching us out. In those beams, I caught the flash of metal from at least two Jerry fighters heading our way. They were the Messerschmitt Bf 110 type we'd encountered before, and they were right on our line of attack. Now I had a choice: flight or fight.

I knew we could outrun them; their top speed couldn't match ours. We weren't there to engage in dogfights. This was no longer a stealth run. The mission had been compromised. There was only one sensible thing to do.

"Abort mission, Ravens, abort," I said, banking away sharply. "Maria, get us the hell out of here."

Maria responded immediately. "Bearing four five zero," she said, taking us on an angle away from the airfield.

"Ravens, full throttle, let's go," I said to the others, aiming to put as much distance between us and the fighters as I could.

"They're still in pursuit," said Pamela as the ground sped by beneath us.

"Keep going," I said. "We'll surely lose them soon."

The beach loomed up very quickly, and I hoped the fighters wouldn't follow us over the water. If they did, we'd be far easier to spot. Jennifer had been shot down over the Channel. I wasn't about to join her. With that in mind, I made a last-minute decision.

"Maria, take us back around," I told her.

"Are you crazy?"

"Do it," I said. "We'll have a better chance of shaking them off."

Maria gave us a new bearing due west. We circled around in a wide arc and then we were heading back the way we came.

"Where are the bandits?" I asked Pamela.

"Still there," she replied.

"Damn it," I said. Then, "Ravens, we'll try evasive tactics. Follow my lead and stay sharp."

I opted to take us in a zig-zag pattern, which made low flying even more hazardous, but there was a chance it would disrupt our pursuers. So far, they hadn't fired on us, but perhaps we were simply not in range. I aimed to keep it that way if I could.

Maria had her eyes trained on the terrain, calling out the hazards.

"Lines."

"Got it."

"Trees, trees…"

"Yes."

"How far to the coast?" I asked Maria.

"Not far, a few minutes."

"All right."

"We're down to one bandit," said Pamela.

Perhaps it was time to turn and fight. The odds would be in our favour, though the other Jerry plane might not be far away. I didn't want to engage the enemy if I could help it. Then an idea came to me.

"Ravens, open your bomb bay doors," I said.

"What are you doing now?" said Maria in alarm.

"Don't worry, I have a plan."

"Oh God, here we go again…" She trailed off.

"Ravens, on my mark throttle back, let the bandit get close, then drop your bombs and go full speed."

"Wilco," came the response.

It was risky, but if I timed it right, we might catch the oncoming Jerry in the blast. At the very least it would disorient him enough for us to get away. We'd be over the coastline soon, and this was our only shot at it.

"Ravens, half-throttle now," I said, cutting the speed. The Mosquito slowed at once.

"Bandit coming up fast," said Pamela. "One minute … thirty seconds … twenty…"

"Bombs away," I said, dropping the ordnance. "Ravens full speed."

I opened up the throttle and the Mosquito lurched forward. The bombs were on fuses of ten seconds, just enough time for us to get clear. If I was right, the Jerry would be caught in the blast zone when they went off. A few seconds later there was a tremendous explosion behind us.

We were just over the coastline when Pamela told us what I had been hoping to hear.

"Bandit has disappeared from the radar," she said.

"Well, I'll be!" said Maria. "You aren't crazy after all."

We both laughed with relief. We crossed the Channel without incident and I was never gladder to see the friendly shores of Blighty come into view.

"Ravens, let's go home," I said.

The mission had failed and that was a worry. How had the Germans detected us? Or were they simply waiting? It was hard to say, but we needed to consider the possibility that they had been forewarned. If that was the case, it didn't bode well for future missions.

I dropped the flight low for the return journey. Although low-level flying had almost become second nature, it was still a hazardous undertaking: inattention at high speed so close to the ground could be fatal.

"Control, this is Raven Leader requesting permission to land," I said as the runway lights at Hawberry came into view.

"You're clear, Raven Leader," said Control.

"Ravens, follow me in."

One by one we landed. I taxied the kite to the standings, then killed the engine.

As we jumped down from the Mosquito, I could see the others were waiting. Sandra looked a little down in the mouth. I knew she would be disappointed that she hadn't been tested in combat.

"Cheer up, chuck," said Maria. "You'll get to kill the enemy another day."

"It's just a letdown, is all," said Sandra. "I was so looking forward to it."

We all laughed at this.

"What?" she said. "I need some excitement in my life."

"You'll get another chance soon enough," I said. "Don't worry about that."

"I sure do hope so," she said.

"Well, *I* thought it was fun," said Lucy, Sandra's navigator.

"Wait until you're really under fire, then you'll have some real fun," said Pamela.

The conversation continued much in the same vein as the truck wended its way back to the Hall. Once there, we made our way to the dining room. Gloria always made sure there were rolls or sandwiches for the returning mission crew. On big missions, there would be a real spread laid on.

After we'd eaten, I went to James's room. I knew he would be waiting.

"How did it go?" he murmured, as I slipped under the covers beside him.

"It didn't. We had to abort," I told him.

"Tell me about it in the morning. I'm just glad you're home safe," he said. Then he wrapped his arms around me and there was no more time for talking.

"This isn't the news we wanted to hear," said Harpo, taking a drag on his cigarette.

Early the following morning, well before breakfast, I was seated at the meeting table in James's office along with the Marx Brothers, Henry, Gloria and James. I had just debriefed them on the failure of the mission.

"Would you have preferred to hear we'd all been killed?" I asked him a little acidly.

"No, of course not that," he replied, not in the least fazed by my tone. "We're glad you made it back. It's just that what you've told us throws up all sorts of questions."

"To which we don't have answers," added his colleague.

"I was thinking the same thing," I said, letting my hackles down a little.

"Do tell," said Chico, tapping out his ash in the ashtray on the table.

"Well," I began, "it almost seemed as if Jerry knew we were coming. We had radar contact with at least two night fighters on our approach, which means they were either scrambled or lying in wait."

"Go on," said Harpo.

"The searchlights came on, on our approach. That's never happened before. We've always taken them by surprise," I continued.

"Why did you decide to abort the mission?" asked Chico.

"Because I didn't think we could successfully carry it out," I said bluntly. "Sure, we've gone in under fire before, but not with fighters waiting to shoot us down."

"FO Nightingale made the right call," James cut in. "We can't risk losing our crew and planes in foolhardy heroics."

Harpo took another pull on his cigarette and blew the smoke out slowly. "You're right, of course. It was the correct decision."

"Thank you," I said, with a tinge of sarcasm.

"We'll be asked these questions by the higher-ups," said Chico, in a more conciliatory fashion.

"Well, you can tell them that we didn't abort because we're women or because we're cowards," I said with some heat.

"We didn't think that," said Chico.

"But others might."

Neither of the Marx Brothers replied to this, but I knew I was right. The Sirens were under scrutiny.

"All right," said James, anxious to move on from what was a contentious topic. "The real question is where does that leave us?"

"It *is* a good question," said Harpo.

"Absolutely spot on," said Chico.

I was a little annoyed by their insouciance, but I knew it was their way. I decided to ignore my irritation and plunge on.

"Do the Germans have radar that can detect our approach at low level?" I asked James.

"Not that we are aware of, no," he replied.

"Then is it possible they knew of our plans?"

"Security here is extremely tight," said Chico. "Also, if they knew that, then they'd know about the Sirens, and if they knew about the Sirens, then…"

"Then we'd know about it too," said Harpo.

"Why do you think that? Wouldn't they keep it secret?" I asked curiously.

"No, we're pretty sure Jerry wouldn't hesitate to try and embarrass the British government by making public the fact that women are flying into combat."

"It would be something of a coup for Hitler, you see," said Chico. "He wouldn't be able to resist it, given that the Reich believes women should remain at home making babies for the glorious future of the Fatherland."

"Then how *did* they know?" asked Gloria, who had been listening to the conversation with interest.

"We don't know," said Harpo. "It's possible they got an inkling of an operation and put all their airbases on high alert without knowing which one we were going to attack."

"But how?" I said, echoing Gloria's question.

"If we knew that, we'd have solved the conundrum," said Chico with a smile.

"We obviously need to ensure that security remains as tight as possible," said James. "That means not mentioning something innocuous in passing to strangers outside the base."

He glanced at me, and I knew he was referring to Shelly. She had let slip that the Sirens was more than just an air transport squadron to a man who had turned out to be a reporter. It had caused a problem at the time.

"Shall I say something to the others?" I asked him.

"Just mention that we need to ensure our secret is safe. Pass the word around and be alert for anything untoward," he replied.

"All right," I said.

"Where does that leave the missions?" asked Henry.

"Good question," James replied and thought for a moment. "I think we'll suspend operations for a little while. Give Jerry the idea we're laying off."

Harpo nodded approval. "Lull them into a false sense of security."

"Precisely," added Chico.

The two spies stubbed out their cigarettes almost in unison and lit up two more. Nobody seemed to have anything more to say.

"If that's all for now, I think we can adjourn for breakfast," said James.

The meeting broke up and we made our way down to the dining room. I was famished, so I helped myself to two slices of toast, beans, eggs and a slice of bacon, since it was on offer.

"Where've *you* been?" asked Shelly suspiciously as I joined the others at our usual table.

"At a debrief," I replied, setting down my plate and proceeding to tuck in.

Shelly, however, wasn't satisfied with that answer. "And how did it go?"

"Stop being so nosey," Maria cut in. "You don't have to know everything."

"I do," Shelly protested. "I can't help it."

"James said we did the right thing, aborting the mission," I told them, waving my fork in their direction.

"Ah, there you go, see … sensible man!" said Shelly at once.

Maria rolled her eyes. I decided I might as well plant the idea of maintaining secrecy there and then.

"Here's the thing: it seemed as if the enemy knew we were coming," I said.

Glances were exchanged around the table, as if someone there had deliberately let something slip. I didn't for a moment think that would be the case.

"So, we need to be sure that we don't say anything, even in casual conversation, to anyone about this unit or about our missions."

"I don't know why you're all looking at me," said Shelly, aggrieved.

"Don't you?" said Pamela at once.

"Well, yes, but I'm not about to be that stupid again, am I?"

"That remains to be seen," said Maria.

"All right, settle down," I said, interrupting this exchange before it became a full-blown argument. "What's in the past is in the past. I'm only concerned that we maintain tight security, all right? Pass the word around, if you will."

"Golly," said Sandra suddenly. "This all sounds so serious."

I regarded her with some interest. "Did you think it wasn't?" I asked.

"No, of course, not. I just … well…" She trailed off.

"This isn't a game," said Maria quietly. "Nobody can know about us. You understand that, right?"

I glanced across at Sandra, but she avoided my gaze. "Yes, of course, of course I do."

Jennifer put her hand on Sandra's shoulder. "It's all right. It's just we're all a bit twitchy, you know, about things like that."

Sandra looked at her gratefully, and the conversation moved on to other things. I hadn't missed the change in Sandra's expression when I was talking about security, however, and wondered if she had said something to someone. Just as Shelly had innocently said something to Gary, the reporter, perhaps Sandra could have done the same. I decided it might be politic to keep an eye on her.

CHAPTER NINE

A couple of days later Sandra once more came to my attention. Our motley crew was passing an afternoon up in my room. Missions had been temporarily suspended, and so we had a little more leisure time than normal.

Jennifer and Connie were sitting by the window, as usual, sharing a cigarette. The rest of us were exchanging childhood anecdotes.

Out of the blue, Susan said, "Where's Sandra?"

I glanced around and sure enough, she wasn't in the room.

"I think she went back to her room," offered Connie.

"How long ago was that?" asked Maria.

"A while ago…" Connie trailed off and continued to smoke her cigarette.

"I think Sandra has a boyfriend," said Shelly suddenly.

"What?" I exclaimed.

Had it not been for what had occurred at breakfast the other day, I wouldn't have thought anything of it. Now, however, my mind was working overtime.

"Why didn't you tell us this before?" said Maria.

"I didn't think it was important and, well, she asked me not to," said Shelly defensively.

"Who is this boyfriend?" I asked Shelly.

"I don't rightly know, but he's off the base… Oh damn!" She looked contrite, no doubt recalling what had happened with Gary.

"For the love of God!" said Maria crossly. "Here we go again."

"Let's not jump to conclusions," I said. "We need to find out more."

"And how are we going to do that, unless we ask her?" said Pamela.

"I guess we're going to have to follow her," I said. I did not like the idea, but the practical part of me told me it was better to be wise before the event rather than after it.

"Yes," said Shelly, sounding excited. "Just like before, when we caught the saboteur."

"Next time Sandra goes out," I continued, "we will follow her. I don't mean all of us — just me and one other, all right?"

"The Boss has spoken," pronounced Shelly in ominous tones.

We all collapsed with laughter and Sandra was soon forgotten about. Now we just had to wait for an opportunity.

Later that night, I spoke to James about it. I decided it was better to tell him before we embarked upon another escapade without his knowledge.

We ate supper together in his private dining room. I enjoyed the time alone with him, doing something quite ordinary. There was roast chicken, potatoes, and rather delicious cooked cabbage.

"Where did you get this chicken?" I asked him, since it wasn't part of our usual fare.

"Ah," he said. "They've been breeding them on the estate, for eggs. This one had stopped laying so..." He trailed off.

"Poor thing," I said, although it didn't stop me enjoying the spoils. I was a farm girl, after all. "I've got something to tell you," I ventured.

"Oh?" James regarded me quizzically.

"We've discovered that Sandra has a boyfriend," I continued, piling some potato and cabbage onto my fork.

"Well, that's hardly a revelation, is it?" he said, then raised an eyebrow when I didn't answer. "Is it?"

"Normally it wouldn't be, but this chap is off the base, and we all remember what happened with Gary."

"Really? You think it could be a repeat of that episode?"

"I don't know. I just have a feeling about it. Besides, shouldn't we follow up on anything untoward?"

"Of course, if you think it's worth pursuing," he said. "Just keep me posted this time — and no more B-17 stunts, if you wouldn't mind."

I laughed and so did he.

"Just let me know," he said, "if it gets dangerous. I'll make sure you are issued with small arms."

I recalled that he had a collection of pistols, which he had handed out to us before. I hoped we wouldn't need them again.

The opportunity to discover who Sandra was meeting came sooner than I expected. I was in my room with Jennifer reading a book when Pamela came rushing in. I had become used to them not knocking and didn't think anything of it. They treated our room like some kind of private clubhouse.

"Sandra…" she said a little breathlessly. She must have run to our room. "She's on the move…"

"What?" I replied, getting up at once.

"She's off somewhere. We need to get after her."

I looked at Jennifer and she nodded. We hurried after Pamela down to the atrium, where we discovered the rest of the gang in a huddle.

"She left on a motorcycle," said Maria.

"A motorcycle?" I said, surprised. "How on earth are we supposed to follow her now?"

"Lucy has gone after her," she told me.

"Lucy can ride as well? And she knows about this? She's Sandra's navigator, for goodness' sake!"

Lucy had not been privy to the previous conversation in my room, for which I was thankful. Loyalty between pilot and navigator was strong. I wasn't sure it was wise for her to be involved at all, but matters had apparently moved on. Shelly decided to add her halfpence worth to the fray.

"It's all right, Boss. She wants to find out about the boyfriend as well."

"God preserve us," I said, annoyed. "Perhaps we should tell the entire squadron about this while we're at it."

Just then, there was the sound of a motorcycle returning. It was Lucy. She switched off the engine, put the bike on its stand and rushed inside to talk to us.

"Sandra's with him now," she said in a loud whisper.

"Where?" said Maria.

"At the Wayfarer's Friend." This was one of the local inns. The others preferred the Dog and Trumpet, though I personally preferred to stay at Hawberry, which had a perfectly good house bar of its own. The fact that Sandra had not chosen the usual haunt made me a little suspicious.

"All right," I said, "I will go with Jennifer and Maria. We'll join them accidentally on purpose and see what's what."

With Jennifer and Maria in tow, I found one of the truck drivers and persuaded him to take us out to the local village. He dropped us outside the Wayfarer's Friend and I asked him to return in an hour. I glanced at the other two as we stood outside the pub.

"Ready?" I asked them.

"Ready," said Jennifer.

We sauntered into the public bar as if we were regulars. A few eyes turned in our direction, but women in uniform were hardly unusual in wartime. The room was quite spacious, with low ceilings and a smoky atmosphere. Jennifer nudged my arm. Over by the window sat Sandra and a man in a suit. We walked over to them and acted surprised.

"Well, hello," said Jennifer. "If it isn't Sandra and…?"

Sandra looked flustered, but the man took the interruption in his stride. He looked to be in his thirties, with blond hair and blue eyes.

"Herman," he said, getting up and making a short, formal bow. "Herman Rakowitz at your service."

"Nice to meet you, Herman," said Jennifer. "I'm Jennifer, and this is Anna and Maria."

"You are colleagues of Sandra?" he asked with interest.

"Anna is my boss," said Sandra, recovering from her surprise.

There was an awkward silence, which was filled by Herman.

"Would you like to join us? If Sandra doesn't mind?" he said, glancing at Sandra.

"Why not?" I agreed, not caring if Sandra minded or not.

"Let me buy you a drink," said Herman.

We didn't demur. I opted for something soft, while the other two requested a half pint of bitter each. Herman went to the bar while we procured some chairs and sat down at the table.

"What are you doing here?" asked Sandra in a low voice. She looked decidedly unhappy at the unexpected turn of events.

"We've come to see who you've been seeing all this time," said Maria lightly.

"There's nothing going on, you know. He's just my boyfriend, that's all," said Sandra hurriedly.

"Did we say there was?" I shot back at once.

"No, but —" Sandra stopped talking as Herman returned with the drinks and sat down. He raised his glass to us and said, "*Na Zdrowie!* That's Polish for cheers."

We toasted him back, and the fact that he'd spoken in what I assumed might be his native language gave me the opening I wanted.

"So, you're Polish?" I asked him.

"Yes, I was born in Warsaw and grew up there, until the war…" He trailed off.

"Herman — that's a German name, isn't it?" asked Jennifer.

He answered this readily enough. "Ah, yes. You see, my mother is German, my father Polish."

Sandra was looking at me and Jennifer with a small frown, which I ignored.

"So, your mother was German," said Maria. "Then you would have been protected from the Nazi regime?"

Herman sighed. "Usually, I would say yes. Except my father was passionately against the Nazis. He did not want to wait and see if my mother's birthright offered us protection. We had already heard of terrible things being done. He decided it would be best for us to leave. My mother's nationality was helpful in that way, to more easily obtain permission and so on. Then, at the last moment, my father decided to stay and fight. So, it was just my mother and I who came to England."

"You didn't want to stay and fight with him?" asked Jennifer, pouncing on this information.

"I wanted to, of course. But my father would not hear of it. He insisted that I look after my mother, so I left."

Herman's explanation sounded plausible; most parents wanted to protect their children from harm.

"And where is your mother now? Is she up here with you?" asked Maria.

"Oh, she is in London. She is safe there. I found a Polish family who she is staying with temporarily," he said.

"All these questions!" Sandra put in suddenly, sounding a little annoyed at our cross-examination.

"It's all right," said Herman. "Your friends are naturally protective. You should be glad."

Despite his reassuring words, I could tell by Sandra's expression that she wasn't mollified at all.

"So you didn't elect to join the forces here in Britain against the Germans?" I asked him.

Herman shrugged and pulled a packet of cigarettes from his pocket. He offered them around and Jennifer took one. He lit hers and then took a long drag on his own before answering.

"I would if I could, but the authorities are naturally suspicious of someone with a German background. So, I'm currently unable to do so."

Once more, this sounded plausible. However, I wasn't finished with my questions.

"Then what brings you here?" I asked him.

"I went up to Cambridge, the university, to see if I can get some administrative work there. I'm waiting to hear from them. I thought I would come and stay a little way out in the country. Then I met Sandra, and I'm sorry to say I've stayed a little longer than I meant to."

"Don't be sorry," said Sandra, reaching out her hand to him. He took it and held it with what seemed to be genuine affection. He took another drag on his cigarette, then turned the subject away from himself.

"Anyway," he said, "you've heard about me — what about you? What brings all of you here?"

"We're transport pilots," I said succinctly.

"Yes, Sandra has told me, but you're with the RAF, no? Isn't it the Air Transport Association who deliver the planes?"

It was said innocently enough, but I was immediately on the alert. I wasn't the only one.

"You seem to know a lot about it, for a layman," said Maria.

"I read the newspapers like everyone else — I like to keep myself informed," he replied without a trace of concern.

"We're WAAFs, to be exact, Women's Auxiliary Air Force," said Jennifer, correcting him.

"And that's all you do? Transport planes?" he asked.

"Sorry to be so boring, but yes," I said. "Oh, we also train pilots and navigators."

I smiled at him disarmingly; two could play this game.

"But you also fly missions from your base, no?" he continued.

"Who told you that?" I asked. The question disturbed me. Someone with only a passing interest would not ask that kind of thing.

"Well ... nobody..." he began.

"I said that I can't meet Herman sometimes because we're confined to the base," put in Sandra.

I did my best not to betray the disquiet that I felt on hearing this. This was exactly what I had been afraid of.

"So, I just assumed..." Herman trailed off.

"Well, we don't," I said with an air of finality. "It's not uncommon for there to be lockdowns on an Air Force base for any number of reasons."

He nodded as if he accepted the explanation and continued to smoke his cigarette. "Security is tight at your base, no?" he said at length.

"Where did you hear that?" Jennifer shot back at him.

"Oh, I've seen the signs and so forth."

"So, you've driven past it?" said Maria.

"Yes, for sure. I did so one time when I was driving around the countryside. I just happened to notice it. Not all air bases are quite as secure…"

He must have seen the scepticism creeping into our faces. He drained his glass suddenly and stubbed out his cigarette.

"I just remembered," he said. "I was supposed to phone my mother. I need to go. I'm sorry."

"Oh, Herman, honey, I thought we were spending the evening together," protested Sandra.

"I'm sorry, *Liebling*, it will have to be another night," he said, standing up.

Sandra stood up too. "Well, at least let me come and say goodbye…"

"Ladies, nice to make your acquaintance," said Herman to us, a little punctiliously. "Come then, *kochanie*…"

I assumed that this was a Polish endearment. We watched the two of them leave the pub. Sandra made a point of putting her hand into his as they did so.

"What do you think?" I asked the others in a low voice.

"*Liebling* is German for darling, isn't it?" said Jennifer. "Not Polish."

"Yes, I noticed that," I said. "We need to get Sandra back to the base, and then I'm getting the Marx Brothers involved. If Herman is a threat to our squadron, then they need to know. I've already told James, in any case."

"Agreed," said Maria, then, "watch out, she's coming back."

Sandra returned to her seat, and I could see there was a defiant spark in her eyes.

"I know what you're thinking," she said as she sat down.

"What are we thinking?" I replied blandly.

"He's not … you know … a spy." She mouthed the last part, fearful of saying it out loud.

"We will discuss this back at base, not here," I said. "We'll finish this drink and when the truck comes to pick us up, you are to follow us back on your motorcycle. Understood?"

"Yes, all right," said Sandra meekly. "But there's nothing wrong with Herman."

"That remains to be seen," I told her.

Shortly after our return to Hawberry, Sandra and I found ourselves seated at the leather-topped table in the room the Marx Brothers used to interrogate people.

Sandra looked, unsurprisingly, a little apprehensive. The Marx Brothers were in no hurry to begin. Instead, they lit up their cigarettes and smoked them unhurriedly. The smoke caught the sunlight coming in through the window.

Eventually, Sandra broke the silence. "Why am I here?" she asked.

"Why do you think you're here?" replied Harpo, batting the question back at her.

"I haven't done anything wrong," said Sandra, sounding a little petulant.

"Haven't you?" said Chico in a disbelieving tone.

"No, I haven't," replied Sandra, beginning to lose her cool. "I'm dating a guy called Herman — what's the problem with that? He hasn't done anything either."

"Hasn't he?" said Harpo with maddening affability.

I remained silent during this exchange. I had witnessed the Marx Brothers' style of interrogation before and knew this was their way.

"No, he hasn't. And if you think Herman is a spy, you're wrong. He's just a guy who came here from Poland, and he hates the Nazis just like everyone else," she blurted out.

"How do you know he's not a spy?" Chico asked, taking a drag on his cigarette.

"I … well … of course, I can't say for certain, but I'm sure he's not." Sandra was starting to sound far less confident.

"His first name is Herman — a German name. His mother is German. He claims his father was Polish, left behind in Poland. You didn't find any of that in the least bit suspicious?" said Chico.

"Well, no… I mean, I thought about it, but he's a good guy. I can tell," said Sandra defensively.

"What exactly did you tell him about the Sirens?" asked Harpo, changing tack.

"Nothing… I just that said I couldn't come out some nights when we were confined to base … you know, because of missions."

"Did you tell him there were missions being operated from this base?" Chico interjected.

"No, of course not! I just said we were not allowed out that night, so I couldn't see him. I didn't mention anything about the missions themselves…" Sandra trailed off lamely.

"And you didn't think he could put two and two together?" Chico continued.

"He did put two and two together," I said, cutting in. "He asked us outright if we flew missions from the base."

The Marx Brothers were aware of the conversation we'd had with Herman in the pub because I had told them about it beforehand.

"On top of which, we understand he showed an extraordinary amount of curiosity about Hawberry," said

Harpo. "He questioned you about the security, for example, admitting that he had driven past it."

"Yes, but surely driving past the base is not a crime," protested Sandra.

Harpo leaned back in his chair and took another drag on his cigarette. "I can't make out, Section Officer, whether you are simply naïve or just plain stupid," he said.

Sandra stood up, pushing her chair back loudly. "I've had enough of this," she said. "I'm not going to stay here a minute longer and endure this horrible way you're questioning me."

The Marx Brothers had deliberately rattled her. This was their way. If something was going to come out, an angry person was far more likely to let it slip. I decided to take a hand in the proceedings.

"Sit down," I said firmly, asserting my authority. "You will remain here until you're dismissed, and that's an order. You are here because this is a very serious matter. This unit is, as you are fully aware, top secret. There have been some attempts to compromise it in the past, and we're not about to allow that to happen again. So, you will tell these chaps what they want to know so we can decide whether or not Herman is a threat to our security."

Sandra sat back down while the Marx Brothers regarded me with something akin to admiration.

"Bravo, Flight Officer," said Harpo.

"Couldn't have put it better myself," said Chico.

"What do you actually know about Herman?" I asked Sandra, a little more gently.

"Well, nothing ... apart from what he's told me," she admitted. Then, from her expression, it seemed as if the penny had finally dropped.

"Damn … what was I thinking? Of course, you're right. I'm just a sucker for a pretty face…"

We couldn't help but laugh at this, which helped to ease the tension in the room.

"You wouldn't be the first," said Chico with a smile.

"What should I do?" asked Sandra. "Should I stop seeing Herman?"

"No," said Harpo. "You should continue to see him, but be very careful about what you say. Take note of the questions he asks you and then report back to us."

"So, you want me to be a spy?" said Sandra, her eyes wide.

"Bingo," said Harpo.

"Got it in one," said Chico.

Sandra clapped her hands together with delight. "How exciting!"

Harpo stubbed out his cigarette in the ashtray. Chico followed suit. They were the ultimate double act.

"Now that we understand each other," said Chico, "we'll leave you to it."

The two of them stood up.

"Toodle pip," said Harpo.

"Chin chin," said Chico.

I watched them leave the room and then turned to Sandra.

"Are you in love with Herman?"

The question had to be asked. Love had been the undoing of many a person. Until James, I hadn't known what love was myself. Even now, I was still unsure.

"No, not in love," she said. "I just have a weakness for blond, blue-eyed boys is all."

"Well, you're going to have to curb it," I said, smiling.

"I see that now." Impulsively she reached out and squeezed my hand. "I'm sorry," she said. "For all the trouble I've caused."

"We all make mistakes, Sandra. It's just whether we learn from them."

"I'm trying," she said in a tone of genuine remorse.

"You're a good pilot," I said. "And you're a Siren now. A sister. All right?"

She smiled on hearing this.

"Come on," I said. "We have to report back to the others."

"Do we have to?" she said.

"No secrets," I told her.

Yet I knew I was keeping the biggest secret of all — my relationship with James.

I left Sandra in my room with the others, who had gathered there in a state of great curiosity.

"You can ask Sandra about what happened," I told them, "but none of this is to go any further than this room, understood?"

"Yes, Boss," said Shelly.

"Moreover," I continued, "I don't want any of you giving her a hard time, or you'll have me to deal with."

Sandra shot me a grateful look. She was already rattled after her interview with the Marx Brothers.

"In the meantime," I continued, "I'm going to report to James."

There was a chorus of 'oohs' from the others, which I studiously ignored.

I found James in his office. He looked up from his desk and smiled when I entered.

"Anna," he said. "What can I do for you?"

I launched right in with a full account of the Marx Brothers' interview with Sandra.

When I had finished, James said, "It does rather sound as if this blighter might be a spy."

"I agree," I said. "But at the moment, we're just keeping him under observation."

"If he knows you're onto him, he could become dangerous," James replied seriously. "I don't want you to take any chances."

I watched curiously as James walked over to a plan chest and pulled open a drawer. Inside were a number of pistols and ammunition.

"Where did you get all of those?" I exclaimed in surprise. I knew that he kept a couple of pistols in his desk drawer, but this was something else entirely.

"I've been thinking about arming the Sirens for a while now," said James. "Take these, but keep them concealed for the moment, if you will."

I could see the genuine concern in his face. On balance, I wasn't averse to having the weapons. If Herman was a spy, it would be perfectly possible that he had a gun himself.

"All right," I said. "I'm going to need ten in that case, plus ammunition."

James procured a tin box with a lid, opened it and proceeded to put the pistols inside, plus several boxes of ammunition. Then he carefully closed it.

"That should do for now," he said.

"I'll take them along to the others," I said, picking up the rather heavy box.

"Until later then, Anna," he said with a disarming smile.

"Yes," I said, smiling back. "Later."

I returned to my room carrying the box. The others were still there and they fell silent as I entered.

"All right," I said. "Now, don't say I never do anything for you."

"As if," snorted Shelly.

I placed the box on the bed and opened it.

"Oh my God!" exclaimed Maria. "Will you look at that!"

"Yes!" said Pamela with relish. "Guns, my favourite!"

"James wants to be sure we're safe," I informed them. "There's one for each of you, including Sandra. You need to keep them concealed."

"Of course, Boss, whatever you say," Pamela said, eagerly taking one of the pistols and starting to load the clip.

"Do I really need this?" Sandra asked me, turning a pistol over in her hand.

"I think you do ... just in case," I told her. I didn't know if any of us would need to use the weapons, but it was just as well to be prepared.

I selected a gun for myself and loaded it methodically. Once everyone was armed, I stowed the tin box away under my bed.

"So, what happens now?" asked Lucy.

"We let Sandra do her job," I said. "And we do ours, if and when the time comes to do it."

"You can count on it," said Pamela, hefting her pistol with satisfaction.

"Just take care of yourself, Sandra," said Jennifer. "And don't hesitate to use that gun if you have to."

Judging by Sandra's expression, she found this a sobering thought.

CHAPTER TEN

The next few days passed without incident. Sandra continued to spend time with Herman, faithfully reporting all that transpired on their dates back to the Marx Brothers. Not long after, she asked to speak to me privately, so we took a walk in the formal gardens. It was a favourite haunt of Jennifer and Connie, where they could be alone. Not many of the staff used the gardens, so it was as good a place as any for a private conversation.

"I'm a little worried, Boss," she began as we strolled down the paths lined with neatly trimmed hedges. The sun was shining and the birds were singing in the trees. It was a beautiful day, almost as if there wasn't a war on at all.

"Oh? Why is that?" I asked her.

"Well, I think Herman might suspect that I'm spying on him." She looked concerned.

"What makes you think he suspects you?"

She hesitated before speaking again. "It's just hard to fake my affection for him knowing what I now know, and I think he's noticed."

"You don't have to do this, you know," I said. "If you are at all uncomfortable, then we should call it a day. I can speak to the Marx Brothers, if you like."

I meant it. Sandra had seemed excited, at first, at the prospect of being a spy, but the reality was somewhat different.

"It's my duty," she said.

"Do you think your life is in danger?" I asked bluntly. "If Herman is a spy, then he could be extremely dangerous. Particularly if he thinks you suspect him."

"No, I don't think that."

"All right, but the moment that you think it is, you need to tell me, and I'll call a halt to it. James will back us up."

Sandra smiled. "Thank you, Boss. And don't worry, I've always got my pistol with me, just in case."

That was true, but I wondered if she had the courage to use it, if it came down to it.

I was on my way back to my room when Judy intercepted me.

"The two gentlemen from MI6 would like to see you, ma'am," she said.

She led me to what now seemed to be their usual room, opened the door and let me in. The Marx Brothers were at their leisure in the armchairs, smoking as usual.

"Ah, Flight Officer," said Harpo.

"Take a seat," said Chico.

I did so and waited patiently while they took several more drags on their smokes. They always did things in their own time.

"We've been looking into Herman's background," said Harpo at length.

"And what have you found?" I asked him.

"Not a lot," said Chico. "And that's what concerns us."

"Oh?" I said, puzzled.

"We can't find any mention of him being a refugee to this country, or his mother."

"If she even exists," added Harpo.

"Are there such records, usually?" I didn't know how the whole administrative thing worked.

"Yes," said Chico. "There have to be immigration papers, visas and so forth."

"I see. So, what are you going to do?" I asked them. "Arrest Herman? Interrogate him?"

"We're not going to do anything," said Harpo.

"Not for the moment, anyway," said Chico. "We want to see how things play out, what he does. We have an operative on his trail now, keeping an eye on him, so to speak."

This was a little comforting, although I wasn't happy that they were leaving Sandra in the line of fire. There was little I could do, however, if that was how they wanted it to go.

"We understand Sandra has a weapon?" said Harpo.

"Yes, we all do," I replied. "She knows how to use it. We've all had small arms training."

"Training is one thing," said Chico. "Shooting a man is another."

"I have to trust that she'll do what she needs to," I said, since I was unable to vouch for her ability in that regard.

"Let's hope so," said Harpo. "Our man will stay as close as he dares. We don't want to spook Herman. He's obviously here for a reason. We want to find out what that is. We also want to know who he's working for, before we make a move."

"He's working for the Germans, surely?" I said, thinking I was stating the obvious.

"Not necessarily," said Chico. "He could be a Soviet spy."

"What?" I said, flabbergasted.

Chico raised an eyebrow. "Did you think Germany was the only country spying on us?"

"Well, yes."

"Far from it. Allies spying on allies. It has been going on for centuries. We're working with the Russians now, but in the future we may not be. So, they spy on us. Stalin notoriously doesn't trust Churchill, or anyone, and especially not the

Americans. So, he wants inside information, to corroborate what we're telling him if nothing else."

"Good God," I said. "I had no idea."

"Wheels within wheels, Flight Officer," said Harpo cryptically. "That's what happens in wartime."

"But why would the Sirens be of interest to the Russians?" I asked him.

"Who knows?" said Chico. "The Russians already have women in combat. It wouldn't be unusual to them. However, perhaps Stalin is looking for leverage. We can't tell why, but we're more interested in who. Who is passing the information to whom."

"And when you have that information?" I prompted.

"Then we can use it to our advantage, to perhaps pass on information we want them to know and information that is not necessarily true, that sort of thing."

"So, a kind of double double cross?"

"Bingo," said Harpo.

"She's got it," said Chico.

I sighed. Given the circumstances, it seemed unlikely they would be deflected from their task.

"As long as you're protecting my Siren, then fine," I replied.

"Rest assured we won't let her come to any harm," said Harpo.

I wasn't quite sure if I believed him. They might not be able to stop it. There seemed to be little I could do about it in any case. I decided not to reveal all of this to the others. It would simply muddy the waters. It was better for them to believe Herman was German and leave it at that. Naturally, I would tell James the whole, if he was not already privy to the information.

"All right, well, thanks for being so candid," I said as I took my leave.

"You're welcome, Flight Officer," said Chico.

"Toodle pip," said Harpo.

Nothing more occurred to cause me any disquiet for several days. We were still being stood down from missions by James. He was taking a precautionary approach to the situation.

In the meantime, I set up a rota to keep watch outside the place where Sandra was meeting Herman. I had run it past the Marx Brothers, since I didn't want to compromise their operation. They had agreed, as long as we were discreet. We used a staff car and followed Sandra when she went out on her motorcycle.

It happened that I was on watch with Jennifer one afternoon. We were sitting in the car a short distance from the Jolly Pirate Hotel, where Sandra was meeting Herman. This was a former coaching inn, where Herman was apparently staying.

"How long do you think this is going to go on for?" said Jennifer. "This Herman thing."

"I have no idea," I replied.

We had been there for an hour and Jennifer was already beginning to yawn, when she suddenly sat up and pointed.

"Look there, it's Sandra — and there's Herman right behind her."

She was right. Sandra was being walked purposefully and rapidly towards our car. She looked scared. Herman had hold of her arm. He was very close behind her and we couldn't see his other hand. Was he holding a gun?

I saw Jennifer reach into her pocket, retrieve her pistol, and cock it.

"Jenny, don't," I said. "We don't know what's going on. Hide that, for God's sake."

Jennifer slid the pistol back into her pocket. By this time, Sandra and Herman had arrived at the car. He wrenched open the back door and shoved her onto the back seat. Then he got in after her, brandishing a gun. Neither Jennifer nor I moved.

"Did you think I didn't know your little game?" he said, pointing the gun at Sandra.

My heart began to race, but I decided the best thing to do was to play for time. Every minute he spent talking was another minute I had to think of a possible way out of the situation.

"What game?" I asked him.

"Do you think I'm stupid? You are watching me, and she — " he indicated Sandra with the barrel of his pistol — "has been playing me for a fool."

"No, Hermie, no," said Sandra *sotto voce*. "I love you, darling, you know that. I don't know why you're doing this."

"Shut up!" said Herman angrily. "Enough of your lies."

Out of the corner of my eye, I saw a man wearing a trench coat and hat. He was standing casually outside the entrance to the hotel, smoking a cigarette. However, I could tell he was surreptitiously observing us. I assumed that it must be the agent the Marx Brothers had spoken of. Herman was thankfully too preoccupied with us to notice.

"Now that you're here, what do you propose to do next?" I asked Herman.

"You are going to drive me to your base," he told me.

"And then?"

"Then I'm going to find out what you are doing there."

"How do you think you're going to do that?" I asked him. "There's one of you and an entire base of personnel."

"Because I am taking Sandra with me as a hostage," he said. "She will lead me to the place where your missions are being planned. If you don't comply, I will shoot her dead."

I almost laughed out loud. It sounded like something out of one of the spy novels I had been so fond of reading as a youth. I couldn't imagine how he thought he would get away with such an absurd scheme.

"You can't possibly get in and out of there alive."

"Oh, but I will, and you will order the others to comply. You are the leader, are you not?"

"Well, yes…"

He had gained a false impression of my position if he thought I held that much sway. However, I didn't like to disabuse him of the notion. Instead, I needed to focus on getting out of this without any of us getting shot or killed.

"Then just do as I say and nobody gets hurt."

"All right," I said. "But I still think you are making a big mistake."

I glanced in the rear-view mirror. Sandra looked frightened.

"Enough talking. Just drive," Herman ordered.

I didn't want to antagonise him further, so I started the car. I pulled out into the road and turned back in the direction of Hawberry. As soon as we started moving, I saw the figure by the hotel set off at a run. He would be following us in short order. As I drove back to the base, I tried to engage Herman in conversation, partly to distract him.

"So, you're a spy, Herman? Who are you working for?"

"It's none of your goddamn business — isn't that what the Americans say?" he shot back.

"Is it the Germans?" I persisted.

"Shut up," he said.

"The Russians?"

"I said shut up!"

I was getting to him, but I didn't want to push him too far in case he did something drastic.

"I was only making conversation," I said, more casually than I felt.

"You British," he said, mocking me. "Always the stiff upper lip. So cool in the face of danger. You think you are superior to the rest of us. Well, you're not."

"You mean like the Fatherland?" I ventured.

"I told you to stop asking questions!" he said, firing up once more.

"Well, then perhaps you mean Stalin?"

He remained silent. I thought perhaps I might have struck a nerve. However, by this time the gates of Hawberry were in sight.

"Say nothing about me to the sentries," said Herman. "And remember, one wrong move and Sandra dies."

So saying, he ducked down in the footwell at the back. I could tell from Sandra's wide eyes that he was still covering her with his pistol.

I stopped at the checkpoint. I was well known to the sentries.

"Drive on through, ma'am," said one of the soldiers after taking a cursory glance at the occupants of the car.

"See how easy that was?" said Herman, sitting up once more. "And the rest will be easy also. If you do what I say, nobody will be harmed."

We drove up the long tree-lined driveway until we arrived at the Hall itself. Herman let out a low whistle.

"I see you ladies are living in style, hmm?"

"We manage," I replied dryly.

He let out a crack of laughter. "One thing I do like about you British is your sense of humour."

I pulled the car up to a stop outside the Hall. "Now what?" I asked him.

I couldn't tell him that as soon as we set foot in the Hall, the rest of our gang would descend on us. All of them were armed. Things could go very badly indeed.

"Where is the mission control room?" he said.

"Inside," I replied vaguely.

"Good, so we will go there together. You will order anyone we meet to stand aside. If you do not, then Sandra will die."

"And just how do you propose to escape?" I asked him.

"Like I said before, that is none of your business."

I didn't think he really had a plan. It seemed inevitable that a showdown of some sort would take place. However, I hadn't counted on Sandra, who suddenly let out a wail.

"Oh, Hermie, you said you loved me, and now look! I can't believe you're doing this to me, to *us*!"

His head whipped around at this unexpected emotional onslaught.

"You don't love me! You never loved me…" She burst into tears. If she was trying to distract him, it worked. It had taken him by surprise.

"Sandra, *Liebchen*, this is not the time … come on … of course I *did* love you, but you were betraying me…"

"See, you *did* love me and now you don't. How could you do this?"

"I have to do my duty… I have a job to do," he said.

"Your duty! Your duty is more important than me?"

"No, wait…" he said as the entire situation rapidly descended into a farce.

It was in that moment that he dropped his guard and lowered his gun, away from Sandra.

Jennifer, who had been watching him closely and waiting for an opening, sprang into action.

The entire scene went into slow motion. In one swift move, Jennifer pulled out her pistol, aimed and fired. Simultaneously, Herman's gun came up and Sandra snatched at his hand, deflecting it as he pulled the trigger. His shot went through the roof. As Jennifer took her shot, Herman opened the car door and rolled backwards out of it. Her bullet went harmlessly into the empty seat.

Before we knew it, Herman was on his feet and looking around for a means of escape. We glanced at each other and on ascertaining that nobody was hurt, we rapidly exited the car. I took my gun from my pocket and so did Sandra. The three of us took aim at Herman.

"Stop!" I shouted. "You are under arrest!"

He turned without hesitation and fired off a couple of rounds. We hit the deck. As I looked up from my prone position, I saw Herman seize a nearby bicycle and peddle off furiously in the direction of the airfield.

"Let's get after him!" I shouted, scrambling to my feet.

"Can't," said Jennifer, pointing at the front tyre.

A stray bullet had punctured it, and it was already almost flat.

"Oh fiddlesticks," said Sandra in exasperation.

"We'll never catch him, not without a car," said Jennifer.

We were wondering what to do, when a black car screeched to a halt next to us. Driving it was the man I'd seen outside the hotel. The MI6 agent.

"Get in!" he shouted.

We piled into his vehicle, and he took off at a tremendous speed in the direction Herman had gone. As we shot off down the road, I saw several Sirens including Shelly, Maria and Patricia streaming out of the Hall. They must have heard the shots.

"Where does this go?" asked the agent, indicating the road ahead.

"The airfield," I told him.

"He's going to steal a plane, most likely," he said. "We have to stop him leaving."

I couldn't imagine a worse scenario than Herman disappearing in one of our planes. No doubt he must be a pilot as well as a spy.

We arrived at the airfield in record time to see the bicycle lying on the ground with the wheels still spinning. Herman was running in the direction of the Spitfire. He heard us coming, stopped, turned and loosed a couple of rounds in our direction. We all ducked down inside the car.

The agent slammed on the brakes as one of the bullets zinged past the windshield. It was no good chasing him like this. I decided to take action.

I flung open the door and jumped out. The others followed suit.

Knowing I was a decent shot, I decided to take a chance. I levelled the pistol and took aim. I fired, one round and then another. Herman pitched forward and went down.

"You got him!" yelled Jennifer.

The agent had joined us. We were about to start walking towards Herman when, remarkably, he dragged himself to his feet and began to limp towards the Spitfire with some determination.

"I've had enough of this. I'm going to take care of it," said Sandra.

Without another word, she set off at a run towards the nearest Mosquito. The rest of us started to move forward warily after the spy, but Herman kept firing the odd shot at us as he went, slowing down our progress.

Finally, he managed to reach the Spitfire and pull himself up onto the wing with difficulty. Then he made it into the cockpit.

"Oh no," said Jennifer. "He's going to get away."

Herman began trying to start up the engine.

"Not if I can help it," I said.

I raised my pistol again to see if I could hit the fuel tank. The other two did likewise. As I was about to pull the trigger, I saw Sandra suddenly reappear from under the Mosquito. She was holding what looked like a grenade in her hand. We kept them in the planes, and she had gone to the Mosquito to retrieve one.

The Merlin engine on the Spitfire caught, just then, and roared to life. Sandra's arm moved in a throwing action, releasing the grenade, which flew in a perfect arc to land in the cockpit of the Spitfire. The last thing I saw before the Spitfire exploded was Herman's startled expression. The next moment, we were all blown off our feet.

"Good God," said the agent as we stood up. "Now I've seen everything."

The Spitfire was burning up. I could hear the sound of the fire tenders rushing to the scene. The cockpit was a complete wreck, and I doubted there would be much left of Herman.

By this time, we had been joined by the rest of the Sirens, Henry, Gloria, James and the Marx Brothers. James came up to me and drew me aside.

"What happened?" he asked.

I told him briefly.

"I'm glad you're all right," he said.

"Yes, I'm all right."

"We'll need a full debrief."

We rejoined the others. Jennifer had just finishing explaining to an interested audience a summary of what had occurred. The Marx Brothers were talking to their fellow agent.

Henry, who had been listening to all of this with interest, turned to Sandra and said with a smile, "You seem determined to destroy that Spitfire one way or another."

"Well, it's pretty much destroyed now," said Sandra, laughing.

"Where did you learn to throw like that?" I asked her.

"Oh, I was in the Ladies Red Stripes baseball team back home. I got a lot of practice."

"All right, I think we've all seen enough," said James. "Let's get back to base."

I accompanied James in his car along with Sandra and the Marx Brothers. They left their fellow agent behind. The others went in the trucks. When we arrived at Hawberry, I located Jennifer, and we went up to James's office. Once there, we sat around the meeting table along with the Marx Brothers, Gloria and Henry.

"Tell us what happened, Sandra, from the beginning," said James.

"Oh, God, sir ... it was just so goddamn awful ... oops."

She clapped a hand to her mouth apologetically. James laughed softly.

"Never mind the protocol," he said. "Just tell us the story."

"All right," said Sandra with a smile. "So, we were in the hotel room, me and Hermie ... I mean, Herman, and he kept looking out of the window. Our room was at the front, you see."

"Damn," I said. "I didn't realise that." I wished I had thought about our surveillance more carefully.

"I should have told you," she said, "but I didn't think he'd notice."

"He's a spy," said Harpo, taking a drag on his cigarette. "*Was* a spy. He would naturally be cautious about his surroundings. But never mind, you weren't to know."

"Go on," James prompted Sandra to continue.

"He became agitated and started asking me why that car was there. I said I didn't know anything about it. Then he started accusing me of lying to him, of pretending to be in love with him. I denied it, of course, but then he suddenly produced a gun."

"I see," said James, who had been listening intently to her story.

"He marched me out to the car with the gun at my back, forced me into the back seat ... and then, well, you know the rest."

I related the events leading up to Herman being blown up in the Spitfire. When James heard about the grenade, he regarded Sandra with interest.

"And you learned to do that playing baseball?" he asked her.

"Yes, I was one of their best outfielders. I can get the ball to any base and land it on a dime. I can pitch pretty well too."

"It was pretty impressive," I added.

"Do you have any idea why Herman suddenly took a pet like that?" asked Chico, leaning back and blowing smoke up into the air.

"No, I don't. I was trying my best to pretend that I still had feelings for him, keep it all like it was before," Sandra told him.

"She's a damn good actress," added Jennifer. "She certainly took him unawares with that performance when we got to Hawberry."

"Oh, that." Sandra laughed. "As well as playing baseball, I also enjoyed amateur dramatics at high school. I can cry on demand…"

We all burst out laughing at this.

"What?" she said. "I'm just being honest."

I could see that Sandra was in her element when she had an audience.

After a few more questions, James ended the debriefing.

"I think we've heard everything we need to hear," he said. "Unless there's anything more?"

"Was Herman working for the Germans or the Russians?" I asked the Marx Brothers.

Harpo took a drag on his cigarette before answering. "We're not entirely sure. We'll be searching his room, of course. Unfortunately, anything useful he had on him will have been incinerated. We also probably won't be able to find his contacts now."

"I'm sorry," said Sandra, looking contrite.

"Don't be," said Chico. "These spies can become a confounded nuisance, so in a way we are happy to be rid of him. We have an inkling it was very possibly the Russians in any case, but as my colleague said, we can't be certain."

"Right then, I will hold a briefing later for the squadron and announce that we can resume flying missions," said James.

"Am I going to have to apologise again?" said Sandra, looking worried.

"No," said James. "Just be more careful about who you pick to go out with in future."

"I will, sir," Sandra said meekly.

"Then I think we're done here. Flight Officer Nightingale, if you wouldn't mind remaining behind?" he said blandly.

"Of course, sir," I replied.

Jennifer threw me a glance before she and the rest of the party took their leave. Then it was just the two of us. James wasted no time in coming around to my side of the table, and in a trice I was in his arms and once more deprived of speech for a very long time.

"You do insist on getting yourself into these awful scrapes," he said at length.

"I'm sorry," I said, not sounding sorry at all.

He laughed. "Don't be. Just make sure you come out of them in one piece."

CHAPTER ELEVEN

Dinner was a raucous affair. Everyone was talking very loudly. I guessed it was the easing of the tension. Even though the spying issue had been known only to a few of us, perhaps the apprehension had been felt by all. Whatever the reason, the squadron was in high spirits.

The usual gang was sitting at our table, consuming a rather nice meal of ham, mashed potatoes and vegetables. There was quite an extensive garden at Hawberry, where a lot of produce was grown to feed the multitude of personnel in residence. Now it was spring, the garden was in full swing.

"You've certainly caused something of a stir since you arrived, Sandra," said Maria.

"It wasn't my intention, I assure you," Sandra replied, tucking into her food.

"Leave her alone," said Shelly. "She's livened things up around here."

"That's one way of putting it," I said wryly.

"I'm sorry, Boss," said Sandra. "For all the trouble I've caused."

"What's done is done," I said. "We can all move on from it and focus on the missions ahead."

"The Boss has —" Shelly started saying.

"Spoken," cut in Pamela. "Yes, we know."

We laughed and I turned my attention to my food, letting the gossip ebb and flow around me.

"I'm surprised you haven't had some entertainment here, with all these people," said Sandra suddenly.

"I thought you *were* the entertainment," quipped Patricia.

Sandra ignored this. "I mean a dance or something, you know."

"Well, we couldn't exactly invite a whole load of outsiders to it," said Connie.

"Yes, but you've got so many personnel on base already — wouldn't it be fun?" Sandra persisted.

"Boss?" said Maria, deferring to me for an opinion.

I put down my fork and thought about it while they all regarded me expectantly.

"I can put it to James and see what he says," I told them.

There was an immediate buzz of excitement. I resolved to speak to James when I had the chance. With dinner over, we filed into the briefing room.

James, Gloria, Henry and the Marx Brothers arrived shortly afterwards.

"I'm sure you're all aware that we were the subject of an attempt to breach our security and discover the purpose of this squadron," said James once we were all seated.

The spying issue was obviously now common knowledge. It would have been impossible to conceal it in any case, considering recent events.

"If we can learn one thing from this," he said, "it's to be very careful about who we associate with."

He glanced at Sandra. She flushed and looked down at the floor.

"You all know how important it is that the truth about the Sirens never gets out. I shouldn't have to remind you that walls have ears. You have to be on your guard, particularly with strangers. Not that I'm forbidding fraternisation with people outside of the base, but I'm asking everyone to exercise even more vigilance from now on. We don't need a repeat of what happened today."

There was silence in the room at his words.

"Moving on to operational matters," he continued. "We will resume Operation Scorpion forthwith. I'm sure you'll be glad to have some action. There is something else in the offing soon, but I can't talk about that just yet. As for the Spitfire, it will be replaced in due course. A new radar-equipped Mosquito will also be delivered shortly, I'm told. So, we'll be up to strength again."

I was pleased to hear this. It would be particularly useful if we ended up flying a full squadron mission again.

"Anyway, that's all for now. The next mission orders will be posted shortly. Dismissed."

As luck would have it, I was chosen to lead the next Operation Scorpion mission against an airbase in France. I decided to give Sandra another shot. The new radar plane arrived and so I elected to take Jennifer too.

The target was an airbase just east of Cherbourg. Although it was apparently a well defended base, it was thought that a small flight of Mosquitos might get through.

"Get in, drop the bombs and get out," Henry had said at the mission briefing. I was only too happy to oblige in that regard. Hanging around German airfields wasn't too healthy for any of us.

The mission was due to fly in the small hours, as usual. I made a point of saying goodbye to James. He had become my talisman, and the feel of his kiss lingered on my lips.

At the appointed hour I walked to the waiting truck with Maria, Jennifer, Shelly, Sandra and Lucy in our flying gear. The night was thankfully clear and there was a partial moon, which would give us some light. Connie came with us to see Jennifer off.

They sat at the back of the truck just as they always did, sharing a cigarette. I tried not to think of the worst on these missions. Every one of us went out with the intention of coming back. I also recalled the terrible feeling I'd had when I'd thought Jennifer was dead. I never wanted to feel like that again.

"Boss," said Sandra suddenly. "Have you spoken to James about the dance?"

I shot her a guilty look, because in truth I had not. The mission had pushed the dance to the back of my mind.

"Not yet — I'm sorry," I told her.

Sandra looked a little disappointed, but then she brightened up. "I could ask him, if you want?"

"No," I said firmly. "I will ask him when we get back, I promise."

"Yes," said Maria. "Let's just concentrate on getting back for now."

The truck arrived at the airfield. We piled out of the back and made our way to the waiting planes. We left Jennifer and Connie to say goodbye to each other.

As we approached the Mosquitos, Victoria appeared out of the shadow of one the wings.

"They're all ready for you, ma'am," she said, snapping a salute.

"Thank you," I said.

"Give Jerry my regards."

She grinned and watched us go to our respective aircraft. I was aware that sometimes the ordnance crew painted messages on the bombs like "This one's for Adolf." I smiled at the thought and wondered what was painted on ours.

I reached our Mosquito and pulled the telescopic ladder down so that I could climb up through the side hatch.

Maria climbed up after me, pulled the hatch shut and strapped herself in.

We looked at each other. It was almost a relief to be flying again. The distractions of the spying business were now behind us.

"Shall we?" I said to Maria.

"Rude not to."

I fired up the engines and they were soon purring nicely. It was a comforting, familiar sound.

"Control, this is Panda Leader requesting clearance," I said over the radio.

Pandas was our codename for the mission.

"Panda Leader, you're clear to go," came the response. "Good luck."

"Roger, thanks," I replied, then, "Panda Flight, check-in."

"Panda One ready," said Jennifer.

"Panda Two ready," said Sandra.

"All right, Pandas, let's do this."

I eased open the throttle and let off the brake, and the Mosquito began to trundle down towards the end of the runway. Once in position, I throttled up the engines. We sped down the runway and were soon airborne. The other two Mosquitos followed in short order.

"Pandas on me, close formation, low level," I said.

Maria gave us the bearing and then the routine kicked in. We were to fly west of London and the Chilterns, then on to Bournemouth, where we'd leave the English coast and head for Cherbourg.

I dropped the plane down low, flicking a glance either side. The others were perfectly in position. Then we were off.

The familiar landscape flashed by beneath us. We'd flown over the environs near the airbase many times before, but Maria still watched our progress like a hawk.

"Lines," she said as I negotiated an almost invisible set of wires.

"Got it, thanks."

I flicked a glance at her and she smiled. Having a second pair of eyes was invaluable.

"House up ahead."

"Seen it."

We flew past Leighton Buzzard, Aylesbury and then Oxford. I thought about the hallowed halls and formidable architecture of the university below us. I had seen pictures, but never visited. I had flown over so much of England but seen very little of it.

"Did you ever want to go to university?" said Maria, picking up on my thoughts.

"It crossed my mind but not in a serious way, and anyway, now we're at war."

"True," she said.

The war had changed everything. All of our futures now depended on winning it.

We arrived over the North Wessex Downs, which were hilly and underpopulated. I put my attention firmly back on the terrain, which undulated quite a bit. Herds of livestock moved in the fields.

"Hill," said Maria.

"Got it."

"Another hill…"

"Yes."

It seemed endless, but we were soon past it and heading towards Salisbury. In the distance I made out the ring of large stones standing dark and tall.

"Isn't that Stonehenge?" said Maria.

"I believe it is."

"I've never been there," she murmured.

As luck would have it, we roared directly over the famous monument.

"Now you have," I told her, laughing.

The easy banter lightened the mood and eased the tension of flying a mission.

Once past Salisbury we turned due south, aiming to pass just west of Bournemouth. The seaside town was in darkness due to the blackout. I tried to imagine what it must have been like before the war, with people on the seafront having fun. We crossed the heathland by Poole and then went over the inky black waters of the Channel.

There were ships below us, probably going to or from the naval base at Portsmouth.

"Pandas, kill the lights," I said, flicking off the navigation lights. "Radars on high alert." Shelly would now be scanning the radar intently for enemy planes. We flew directly for Cherbourg on the bearing Maria gave us. It was a straight run passing east of the town and straight onwards to the airbase. We'd be on an attack run almost as soon as we hit the French coast.

"Showground in ten," said Maria, indicating the time to the target.

"Roger," I replied. "Keep it tight now."

Another five minutes sped by. We could see the white outline of the shore ahead. Suddenly, the radio crackled to life.

"This is Panda One, radar contact — several bandits," said Shelly.

This was not good news.

"How many, Panda One?" I said at once.

"I don't know, loads, I mean... Jesus Christ!"

The world exploded in front of us as the airbase was lit up by ordnance. Tracers were streaming out into the darkness.

"What the hell is going on?" said Maria.

I had no idea, but I kept going. We needed to get nearer to find out what was happening.

"Pandas stay on course," I said, slipping off the safety on the guns.

"We're closing in on the bandits," said Shelly as the airbase loomed closer.

Then suddenly we saw them.

"Those aren't bandits," said Maria. "Those are ours."

Sure enough, in the glow of the fires we could clearly see a number of Mosquitos flying in against the target, one after the other — exactly as we had been trained to do.

"What do we do, Panda Leader?" said Jennifer. We were now closing rapidly with the target.

I thought quickly. We could join in, but we were not in radio contact with whoever this squadron was. They'd already alerted the Germans and there was a great deal of enemy fire coming from the base. It wasn't a situation I wanted to get into. I made a decision. I banked away from the airbase in a tight turn.

"Abort mission, abort," I said, the words sounding hollow in my own ears.

"Are you serious?" said Sandra.

"Abort, Panda Two, that's an order. Maria, give us a bearing for home."

"Roger," said Maria.

Within a short space of time, we were headed back to Bournemouth at full throttle. I was anxious to be gone before the other Mosquitos broke off their attack. They would inevitably want to know who we were, and I wouldn't be able to tell them. Also, we were on a completely different radio frequency to other Allied aircraft, for obvious reasons.

"Who the hell *were* they?" said Maria, once we were safely over the water.

"I have no idea," I replied. I just knew that someone must have known that the target was designated for the Sirens and nobody else should have been attacking it at the same time.

"Whoever they were, they had no business attacking our target," said Maria hotly.

"I'm sure James won't be happy when he finds out," I said.

"*I'm* not bloody well happy," said Maria.

"I don't think any of us are," I said.

I was sure Sandra would be disappointed. Her second mission, and she had been thwarted yet again.

"Here comes Bournemouth," said Maria, putting her mind back on the job.

We flew home the same way we'd come. Even the sight of Stonehenge now bathed in moonlight did little to cheer us up. This was my second mission in a row that I had been unable to complete.

"It's not your fault, so don't even think it," said Maria, who seemed to be able to read my mind.

"I guess not…"

"I know not. Mistakes happen and that's all," she said with an air of finality.

"Yes, Mum," I quipped.

"You can stop that and all," she said, laughing.

In what seemed like no time at all, the airfield at Hawberry loomed up ahead.

"Control, this is Panda Leader requesting clearance to land," I said.

"Roger, you're clear," said Control.

I lowered the undercarriage as the runway lights came on. I eased the Mosquito down and taxied to our standing. Once we'd stopped, I killed the engine.

"Come on," said Maria. "Let's get a cup of cocoa."

"Yes," I said. "Hopefully there are some sandwiches too." We were always hungry when we got back from a mission.

We jumped down from the plane and were met by the others. As we stood waiting for the truck, Sandra voiced her disappointment.

"This is worse than being stood up on a date," she said.

We all laughed.

"It's the luck of the draw," I told her.

"Well, maybe it's me. Maybe I'm the jinx."

"Don't start talking like that," said Shelly, cutting in. "This isn't your fault."

"You're one of us now, Sandra," said Jennifer. "For better or for worse."

"Gosh, it sounds like a marriage," said Sandra.

"Once a Siren, always a Siren," I said.

The truck arrived and Connie jumped down from the back.

"So," she said, "how was it?"

We all burst out laughing.

Unusually, James came down to the dining room where we were drinking cocoa and munching on cheese sandwiches.

"How was the mission?" he asked me.

"We aborted," I told him.

"What? Why?"

"Someone else was there before us," I said, and gave a brief explanation of what had happened.

James suddenly looked rather grim. "I see," he said.

"Do you have any idea who they might have been?" I asked.

"No, but I intend to find out," he said. He turned to the others. "I will sort this mess out tomorrow. Get some sleep, all of you." Then turned on his heel and left.

I did not miss the fleeting look in his eyes that told me he hoped to see me later. I resolved to go to him as soon as I could.

I sipped my cocoa. James was a Wing Commander, but there were several ranks above his. He wouldn't be able to get too shirty with the top brass. I wondered how the mix-up had occurred, if indeed it was a mix-up. My thoughts raced. James had said there were detractors. What if someone had deliberately ordered a strike on the same night as ours?

"Go to bed, Anna," said Maria, coming up to me. "You need it; we all need it."

Jennifer and Connie had already disappeared together. The others finished their food and then took their leave. Then it was just me and Maria.

"I've seen how he looks at you," she said softly.

"What?"

"His eyes light up, Anna. Don't tell me you haven't noticed."

"I don't know what to do, Maria. I mean … it's complicated."

"Is it? Or are you just making it that way?"

I stared at her. "I just don't know what other people would think…" I trailed off.

"This isn't about other people," she said. "It's about you, and when you work out what's holding you back, I'm sure you'll know what to do."

I set down my empty cup.

"Go on," she said with a smirk. "Go to him … and try to get some sleep too."

I turned and gave her a spontaneous hug. "What would I do without you?" I whispered.

"Be like a ship lost at sea, probably," she said, laughing.

"Well, you are a navigator."

"Go!" she urged, shooing me out of the dining room.

I went to my room and got changed out of my flying gear. Then I wended my way quietly through the now familiar corridors to James's room and let myself in.

James was in bed. He smiled when he saw me. I slipped in beside him and he enfolded me in an embrace.

"What are you going to do about the mission?" I whispered.

"Right now, nothing," he replied. "Tonight I've got something far more important to do."

"Oh? And what's that?"

His lips touched mine and there was no more time for talking.

I returned to my room in the early hours, climbed into bed and snuggled up to Jennifer. She stirred softly but didn't wake.

At breakfast, all the talk at our table was about the mission.

"Who the hell ordered a strike on the same airbase on the same night?" asked Patricia indignantly.

"That's what James is going to find out," I said.

"Well, I hope he gives them a piece of his mind," said Pamela. "I would certainly like to."

I held my peace. We'd know soon enough. The other Sirens weren't fully aware of how precarious our position was at times. It was almost as if we had to prove ourselves to be twice as good as the male pilots.

With breakfast over, I went upstairs to James's office. I knocked on the door and entered. He was sitting at his desk, putting down the phone. The expression on his face told me all was not well.

"What happened?" I asked as I approached. "Is it bad news?"

James let out a big sigh. It wasn't like him to be quite so despondent.

"It's not bad news, precisely; it's just not the news I wanted to hear."

"Oh?"

He got up and paced the room in an agitated fashion. "There is a secret protocol for our missions. When we've a mission allocated, just like any other squadron, nobody else is supposed to touch it or the target. Certainly not on the very same night that we attack it."

"So, what went wrong?" I asked, puzzled.

"Someone decided not to follow protocol. They overrode the mission orders and took on the mission without informing us, making us look like a pack of bloody fools."

"Oh!"

"And that," he said, "was precisely the intention."

I frowned. "But surely if they broke protocol, then they should be getting a slap on the wrist or something, shouldn't they?"

James shook his head. "Ordinarily, yes. However, this chap is holding sway at the moment and for whatever reason, nobody is inclined to do anything about it."

"Who is this chap?" I asked. "How come he's immune to criticism for his actions?"

"Air Commodore Christopher Laxington," he said.

The name didn't ring a bell.

James sighed again and resumed his seat. "Do you remember when I said that there were some detractors?"

"Yes," I replied. I recalled this very well.

"Well, he's one of them."

"All right, but Air Commodore isn't that high up, is it? There are others above him, aren't there?" I asked.

"Yes, there are, but currently his star is somehow in the ascendent."

"And ours is on the way down?" I guessed.

He didn't reply, and I knew that I was near the mark.

"I've been told that while my mission slots are supposedly sacrosanct, they can no longer be guaranteed. If, for example, someone like Laxington wants to fly his favourite team instead, then we are to defer to him."

"What?" I was flabbergasted. "That can't be right, surely? We've been doing a great job. You said so yourself."

James's voice was filled with bitterness. He'd gambled his entire career on the Sirens. "We have, and we are. And we will continue to do a good job for as long as we're allowed to do it."

"What are you saying, James? That this is the end of the Sirens?"

"I am going to do everything in my power to keep the Sirens flying. Believe me when I say I'm not going down without a fight," he said grimly.

"*We* are not going down without a fight!" I told him. "You have the Sirens at your back, and we are not to be underestimated by anyone."

"Thank you," said James. "And now, if you'll excuse me, I had best talk to Henry and Gloria. We'll put our heads together."

"All right."

I left his office and went to round up the gang. We'd put our heads together too — then we'd see about Air Commodore Laxington.

When I told the others, there was outrage and indignation at once.

"Who the bloody hell is this bloody charlatan?" said Shelly, firing up.

"How dare he?" added Susan hotly.

"I would like to give him something to think about," Maria said, balling up her fists.

"What did you say his name was?" asked Sandra. "Laxative or something?"

We all burst out laughing.

"Laxington, silly," said Jennifer.

"It's Air Commodore Christopher Laxington," I said as the mirth subsided.

"Is he trying to disband the Sirens?" asked Shelly.

There was silence and everyone looked me.

I shrugged. "I don't know," I said. "James didn't precisely say that."

"Well, how can he? Can't James just go over his head?" said Maria.

"Look, for some reason Laxington's being given a lot of credence with the top brass. No idea why. Apparently, he doesn't like the Sirens... James says he's a detractor."

"So what can we do about it?" asked Connie.

It seemed hopeless, but I felt there must surely be a way around it.

"I don't know — I need time to think," I replied.

"Sounds like another B-17 job," said Pamela.

"We cannot drop a senior officer in the RAF out of a B-17," I told her severely. "Besides which, we'd all end up on the gallows or in front of a firing squad."

"Not if we said that he slipped," Pamela murmured darkly.

I shook my head. "I'm asking for sensible solutions."

Jennifer took a drag on her cigarette and handed it to Connie. They were sitting by the window as usual.

"Let's all just calm down a little," she said. "We don't even know what we're dealing with yet. The best thing we can do, for the moment, is do our jobs and do them well."

I smiled at her and she smiled back.

"Jenny is right," I said. "We might never hear from Laxington again."

CHAPTER TWELVE

Two days after our conversation, a staff car arrived at Hawberry Hall. In it was Air Commodore Christopher Laxington himself. I happened to be talking to the receptionist, Sergeant Martha Pryde, when he marched up to the desk.

He was a rather portly man, with a shaved head on which he wore an officers' cap, which sported a line of braid. His ill-fitting jacket also had braided epaulets befitting his rank. Following him closely was a Section Officer with mousy brown hair and brown eyes. I assumed she was his adjutant.

I snapped to attention and saluted, as did Martha. Laxington scarcely afforded me a glance.

"Air Commodore Laxington," he said, announcing himself rather pompously. "This is my adjutant, Section Officer Sally Green. I'm here to see Wing Commander Donnington. We'll also both need quarters for the night, if not longer."

"Yes, sir," said Martha. "I will call the Wing Commander's adjutant to take you to his office, and then I will sort out your quarters."

"Excellent, good girl," he said.

This got my back up immediately. I didn't know whether to stay or go, so I waited, since as far as Laxington was concerned I was part of the background furniture in any case.

"So, this is the Sirens, is it?" he murmured to no one in particular as Martha spoke to Judy on the phone. "All this for one bloody squadron," he continued, looking around the atrium with a jaundiced eye. "Shocking waste of money."

I suppressed my murderous thoughts with an effort.

After an awkward silence Judy appeared, hurrying down the corridor. She snapped a smart salute, and Laxington returned a perfunctory one.

"I'll take you to the Wing Commander now, Air Commodore," said Judy.

"Very good, lead the way," said Laxington, already acting as if he owned the place.

The two newcomers disappeared with Judy, and I glanced at Martha. She was quietly smouldering with suppressed anger.

"I'd best go and see to his *quarters*," she said through gritted teeth. "Good girl, indeed!"

I watched her walk away and then I headed for James's office. I had no idea what I was going to do there, but I wanted to know what was going on. As I approached the closed door, I could hear raised voices from within. I stood a little to the side of the door and listened intently.

"You've come here, unannounced, sir, to do an inspection. Is that what you're telling me?" said James.

"What I'm telling you is that your outfit is haemorrhaging money, and the RAF is paying for it. I want to know why and I'm going to find out," said Laxington.

"The Sirens has been sanctioned by the highest authority. We are doing a sterling job flying dangerous missions very successfully."

"From what I hear, not *all* are successful; you aborted the last two," Laxington shot back.

"One of them was because your squadron had usurped our target!" said James angrily.

"Usurped? Please remember you are speaking to a senior officer," Laxington retorted.

"Just why are you here, sir?" James demanded. "What are your intentions towards this unit?"

As I waited to hear the answer, I found Judy at my elbow. She had arrived so quietly I hadn't noticed. Judy smiled and raised a finger to her lips. Laxington's next words were chilling.

"I'm here, Wing Commander, to shut this unit down. And I will do it, one way or another."

"You can try, sir, but I will fight you all the way to Churchill if I have to," said James.

"Your days are numbered, Wing Commander, as are the days of the Sirens. The days of treating the RAF like an open chequebook are over. I'm going to see to it that you are held to account for your actions."

James lost his temper. "What bloody actions, sir? Helping to win this bloody war? Are those the actions you're talking about? I've got a crack unit who have carried out successful raids on the enemy and inflicted considerable damage. You've got a damn nerve coming here and telling me that you're going to hold us to account. Just because you've got some damned old-fashioned notion about women in combat, it doesn't give you the right to shut down this unit."

"And you've got some nerve talking to me like that. It's insubordination. Women don't belong in combat!"

There was an ominous silence. I wondered what was going on. I imagined James was controlling himself with an effort.

"You will arrange a briefing where I can address your squadron myself and put them on notice. I also want a tour of all the facilities, including the airfield. Do I make myself clear?"

"Yes, sir, I will see to it," said James, sounding defeated.

"I will see myself out. Let me know when the briefing is to be held," said Laxington.

I heard his footsteps approaching the door. Judy jerked her head, indicating that I should make myself scarce. I left her to it and hurried away down the corridor.

"This way, sir," I heard Judy saying. "I'll show you to your quarters."

As their footsteps receded, I returned to James's office and opened the door. He was sitting on the sofa with his head in his hands. I shut the door and went to him immediately. I sat down and put my arms around him.

"Darling," I said, "please don't be upset. There's got to be a way out of this."

"You don't know what Laxington just told me," he said, looking at me in despair.

"Actually, I do," I replied. "I was listening at the door."

He looked at me with a flash of amusement. "Were you really?"

"Yes, I'm sorry. Laxington arrived while I was talking to Martha. He didn't even notice me. So, I followed him up…"

"And you thought you'd come and listen to my private conversation?" he said, a smile playing on his lips.

"Yes, I did."

"So you will have heard what he said about shutting us down."

I stared at him. "Are you really going to let him do that without a fight?"

He sighed. "I'm not saying that, no. I'm just damned if I know *how* to fight it, Anna. I've been fighting this battle for a long time. I'm starting to feel like I'm running out of options."

"Well, I'm not giving up," I said firmly. "There has to be a way to stop him."

"I hope you're right," said James. I'd never heard him sound quite so despondent.

My next port of call was the Marx Brothers. I had no idea how I would prevent Laxington from shutting down the Sirens, but

I was determined to try. I decided that I would see if I could enlist their aid. They were often rather elusive, but a quick word with Martha informed me of their whereabouts. They apparently had their own office in a little-used wing of the Hall. I made my way there and knocked on the door. It was opened by Harpo, who had a cigarette hanging out of his mouth. Unusually, he was in shirtsleeves.

"Flight Officer, you managed to track us down to our humble abode. Do come in," he said, holding the door open.

I entered to find a plush room in keeping with the rest of the mansion. Apart from various pieces of antique furniture, it also had a couple of desks, filing cabinets, and a table covered with neat piles of light brown folders marked 'Top Secret'.

"Welcome to our home from home," said Chico, setting aside a file he had been reading.

"Seat?" said Harpo, indicating an empty chair.

I sat down and Harpo did too. The two of them regarded me with interest whilst smoking their cigarettes. The smoke danced in the sunlight coming through a large window, the upper part of which was stained glass, sending streaks of colour around the room.

"What brings you here?" asked Harpo after a moment.

"Air Commodore Laxington," I began.

"Ah," said Chico.

"He's here," I said.

"Yes," said Harpo.

Naturally they would know, although I had no idea exactly how. They seemed to know everything that went on.

"He wants to shut down the Sirens," I said. "Can he do that?"

"Well," said Harpo, "he *thinks* he can do that."

"But can he?" I persisted.

"Technically, he might," said Chico. "But we're working on it so that he can't."

"How?" I demanded.

"It's tricky," said Harpo.

This was no more than I might have expected from them. They seemed to talk in riddles quite often.

"Look," I replied, a little exasperated, "I want to help. What can I do? What can *we* do, me and my crew?"

"Laxington has the ability to cause us a lot of trouble and extra work to prevent him from shutting this place down. At the moment, it's best to play along while we put things in motion, if you get my drift?"

"Oh! Lull him into a false sense of security, you mean?" I said, cottoning on.

"Something like that, yes," said Chico.

"And then we strike?" I asked hopefully.

"That's the part we're working on, but if you've a way to short-circuit the process, then all to the good," said Harpo.

I sighed. This wasn't really helpful at all. If the Marx Brothers didn't have the answers, then who would have them? Of course, it was hard to tell with these two. I realised the conversation wasn't getting me anywhere.

"All right, well, I will go and see what I can come up with."

"That's the ticket," said Chico.

"Toodle pip," said Harpo.

I left their office no further forward. However, as I arrived back at my room, I ran into Jennifer and Connie.

"A briefing has just been called," said Jennifer.

My heart sank. "All right," I said. "I suppose we'd better go then."

We assembled as usual in the briefing room and waited.

"I wonder what it's about?" said Shelly.

Maria glanced at me. "You know, don't you?" she said quietly.

"You'll find out," I said. It wouldn't do to spread alarm. Laxington would do that soon enough.

"Attention," said Gloria, entering the room.

We all stood up while James, Henry, Gloria, Laxington and Sally followed her in and took to the podium. I noticed the absence of the Marx Brothers and wondered if they'd stayed away on purpose. Perhaps they did not wish to alert Laxington to their presence.

"Who's that?" hissed Shelly.

"Hush," Maria admonished her.

She glanced at me again. I looked back helplessly. Trouble had arrived at the Sirens with a capital T.

"At ease," said James. Once we were all seated, he continued. "I would like to introduce Air Commodore Laxington, from Bomber Command, who would like to say a few words."

Laxington stepped forward and removed his cap. Looking at his egg-shaped head and rotund frame, I couldn't help but think of the nursery rhyme about Humpty Dumpty.

"Hello," said Laxington. "So, this is the Sirens. Very impressive, very impressive indeed."

He paused and looked around, smiling. There were several tentative smiles from the Sirens, but I knew that this was simply his way of softening us up. Laxington was about to disabuse us of any notion that he was here to tell us what a great job we were doing.

"Yes," he continued. "Highly impressive to see women flying missions on the front line in this fashion."

I noticed the smiles turn to puzzlement.

"Yes, indeed. But it is also a highly unusual setup. An experiment, one might call it. And one which is soon to come to an end."

There were audible gasps at this, but Laxington was in full flow.

"I am not the only one in the top echelons of the RAF who believes that women should not be in combat. It's a man's job. In fact, one might say it should be *exclusively* a man's job. Combat is no place for women. I intend to ensure that the mistake that has been perpetrated by bringing this unit into existence will be corrected."

The puzzled frowns had turned to scowls in very short order. Laxington seemed oblivious, however, to the mood of the room.

"I am here to do an inspection and report on this squadron. I'm pretty sure that I will find that the expense of keeping this unit flying could have been better spent elsewhere on combat units flown by men. And if, as I expect, those are my findings, I shall be recommending that this unit is shut down ... for good."

Many of the Sirens were staring at him in open disbelief.

"I think it's only fair to give you warning. You will all be reassigned to roles which are appropriate to your positions as *women* in the Air Force. That will be all."

Without another word, he put on his cap and left the room with Sally in tow. As soon as he was gone, the room filled with the buzz of angry voices. Everyone started talking at once.

Maria looked at me, her eyes full of fury. "How dare he?" she growled. "How bloody well dare he come here and say that!"

I reached out my hand to her. "We've got to find a way to stop him," I said quietly.

James let the uproar go on for a few moments and then he called for hush. The room became silent, although the mood didn't change.

"Air Commodore Laxington is currently the senior officer on this base, and we are duty-bound to treat him with the respect his rank demands," he said. "However, for the record, I don't agree with anything that has been said."

"Too bloody right!" said Shelly.

James smiled. "Listen," he continued, "we are the Sirens. We do not go down without a fight. First of all, let's show Laxington that we're the smartest unit in the Royal Air Force. Let's show him what we're made of. Rest assured I am doing everything I can to ensure that what he's just told you does not come to pass. We will prevail!"

It was a stirring speech. From somewhere at the back, someone started up a chant.

"Sirens, Sirens, Sirens…"

It was taken up on every pair of lips like a war cry, every voice in the room thundering it out.

"Sirens, Sirens, Sirens…"

It was the sound of thirty-six women ready to fight for their survival. The survival of the Sirens.

My room had now become the 'War Room', where all the usual gang were gathered.

"I can't believe this is happening," said Susan. "After all we've been through — to get disbanded for no good reason."

"The reason is the whim of one selfish man," said Connie.

"He needs to be stopped," added Pamela.

"Pamela," I said firmly, "I don't want to hear anything about a B-17."

"I wasn't going to mention it," Pamela said with a mock pout.

"How are we going to stop this happening?" said Patricia, ignoring this exchange. "Does anyone have any actual ideas?"

There was silence. Laxington was top brass, or close to it. What could any of us do against him?

"Does anyone know someone of a higher rank than him?" said Sandra. "Someone who might be on our side?"

I shook my head. "I think that's more the Marx Brothers' domain."

"Well," she continued, "there's only one thing for it then."

All eyes were turned towards Sandra with great interest.

"And what's that?" said Maria sceptically.

"We need to set up a honey trap," said Sandra, smiling.

"A what?" said Shelly with a puzzled expression.

"You've never heard of a honey trap?" Sandra glanced around at our blank expressions. "Listen, if you want to catch a pest, you've got to put down some honey, so…"

"So, we lure him into a compromising situation," said Jennifer, catching on fast.

"You've got it," said Sandra.

"All right, but how do we do that?" asked Lucy.

"Well, we need to find someone attractive, who can make herself irresistible…" Sandra trailed off because we were all looking at her.

"And you, Sandra," said Maria, "are perfect for the role."

"What, little old me?" said Sandra, trying to put on an innocent expression.

"I can't think of anyone more fitting, frankly," I said.

"And you know it," added Connie with a tinge of sarcasm.

"All right," said Patricia, "but assuming you can lure Laxington into this trap, what happens then?"

"Well, then we've got to gather some evidence against him," said Sandra. "To make him see sense."

"Blackmail him, you mean?" said Pamela.

"Blackmail is such an ugly word, don't you think?" said Sandra. "Think of it more as persuasion."

I regarded her with newfound respect. "I'm surprised that you're not working for the Marx Brothers," I said.

"I like flying too much to be a spy," said Sandra. "Although I'd probably be good at it."

"A femme fatale and no mistake," said Maria.

"Talking of the Marx Brothers," put in Jennifer, "they would know how to get the evidence."

"Good point," I replied. "I will go and talk to them about it now. In the meantime, the rest of you can discuss how this plan could work. After all, luring Laxington into a compromising situation might not be all that easy."

"Oh, believe me, I know his type. It would be like taking candy from a baby," said Sandra.

"All right, well, I'll be back. Behave yourselves until then," I said with a grin as I left the room.

There was a chorus of "Yes, Boss" as I closed the door. I made my way rapidly to the Marx Brothers' office with new hope in my breast.

Harpo opened the door and bade me sit down. The two of them were smoking cigarettes as usual and looking perfectly at their ease. This irked me somewhat, considering the predicament we were in.

"Flight Officer," said Harpo. "What brings you here?"

I refrained from rolling my eyes at this, since they must have known exactly why I had come to see them.

"You've no doubt heard what Laxington said at the briefing," I replied.

"Alas, we have," said Chico.

"And?"

"We're working on it, as we said before," said Harpo, taking another drag from his cigarette and blowing the smoke up into the air.

"Well, we've come up with an idea," I said, since they were not being very forthcoming.

"Do tell," said Chico.

"It was Sandra's idea, actually, involving what she calls a 'honey trap'…"

I went on to explain what it was, and the two spies cottoned on pretty quickly.

"Ah, yes," said Harpo. "A common tactic used in spying circles to persuade someone to become more cooperative."

"Oh good," I said. "So, you know all about it."

"Yes, indeed we do," said Chico.

I could well imagine that they had probably employed exactly that tactic. I wondered why they hadn't come up with the idea themselves, in that case. However, it wasn't the time to dwell on such matters.

"So, what do you think?" I asked them.

"Sounds like a good plan," said Harpo.

"Which certainly might work," said Chico.

"All right, good. I was hoping you might have some ideas about getting the evidence of the compromising situation," I said.

Harpo and Chico said nothing for a few moments. They finished their cigarettes, stubbed them out and lit up two more. I waited a little impatiently, knowing they could not be rushed.

"Well," said Harpo at length, "there are two main forms of evidence one can obtain, the first being photographs and the second being secret recordings."

"Go on," I said.

"The problem with photographs is obviously that the victim, as it were, has to be either secretly photographed or given something to help them sleep, while the compromising photographs are taken. They are hardly likely to allow anyone to photograph them otherwise."

"Yes, I see," I said.

"The secret recordings are easy enough," said Chico. "Just conceal a microphone in the room and Bob's your uncle."

"And afterwards?" I asked him. "Once we have the evidence?"

"You leave that part to us. We will deal with Laxington," said Harpo in slightly ominous tones.

"There are a few matters that need to be sorted out, however," said Chico.

"Oh?"

"A suitable location for the seduction, and of course a suitable potion to put Laxington to sleep. Fortunately, we can supply the requisite potion — a clear liquid, undetectable, very fast acting."

"He'll go out like a light," added Harpo.

"All right, but I assume we will have to sort out the location and a way of getting him to it," I said.

"Precisely," said Harpo.

"Indubitably," said Chico.

"Then I'd best get planning," I said as I took my leave.

I returned to our temporary War Room in a pensive mood. Though the plan had merits, getting Laxington somewhere where it could be carried out would be quite a feat. I knew I should tell James, but I was in two minds about that, because he might not approve.

With these and other thoughts running through my head, I entered my room to something of a surprise. The last person I'd expected to see was Laxington's adjutant, Sally Green.

The others were nowhere to be seen, and Sally was sitting in one of our armchairs with her hands folded in her lap.

"What are you doing here?" I asked her.

"I wanted to talk to you," she said.

"Where are the others?"

"They left so that I could talk to you alone. At my request."

"All right," I said, sitting down on the bed. "What did you want to say to me?"

Sally hesitated, and then it all came out in a rush. "I wanted to tell you that I don't agree with what Air Commodore Laxington is doing. I don't agree with it at all. He's an awful man and so overbearing. He orders me around like a servant, and I'm not... Anyway, I just wanted you to know, so you didn't think I was part of it. I wish I could do what you do, flying into combat. It sounds so exciting..." She trailed off, looking despondent.

I suddenly saw an opportunity. "Sally," I said tentatively, "would you ... help us?"

She looked at me for a moment, and I wondered if I'd made a mistake in asking.

"I don't really see how I can," she replied.

"What if we had a plan to save the Sirens? Would you help?"

She regarded me earnestly. "Tell me what I can do, and I'll do it. If there's a way to stop him, then count me in."

"All right," I said. "That's good to know. We still have to work things out, but let me go and find the others."

I went to the door and opened it. The rest of the gang practically fell into the room. They'd been waiting outside.

"Honestly!" I said to them. "What are you like?"

"We were listening," said Pamela.

"I would never have guessed," I said sardonically.

"Anyway," said Maria, "we've got an even bigger surprise for you."

"Oh?"

They all stood aside and ASO Diana Fletcher stepped forward. She had blonde curly hair, blue eyes and a bow mouth. She reminded me a little of Sandra.

"Diana, is it?" I asked her.

"Yes, ma'am," she said, saluting.

"Has she got a tale to tell you," said Shelly in the manner of a ringmaster introducing their favourite circus act.

"Sit down then, Diana. Don't stand on ceremony. What is it you want to say?" I said to her.

The rest of the gang disposed themselves comfortably around the room, on the beds or chairs, leaving Diana standing up and holding court.

"When I first saw Laxington, I thought I recognised him," she began. "And then I became very sure."

"Recognised him from where?" I asked her.

"Wait until you hear this," interjected Shelly.

"Hush, let Diana tell it," said Maria.

Shelly made a face at her but subsided.

"Not long ago, before I became part of the Sirens, I was … well, what I'd call an 'escort companion'," Diana continued. "That's a person who spends time with men … you know, for money."

"So let me guess," I said. "One of these men was Laxington?"

"Yes," she said. "He was very generous with his money. Let's say he had some unusual tastes … which, as a consequence of his generosity, I was happy to indulge."

153

"Oh?" I wasn't sure I wanted to know about these unusual tastes, but Diana continued anyway.

"He liked to be tied up … called names… He enjoyed…"

"Yes," I said, holding up my hand. "I think I get the gist."

"You probably think I'm an awful person, ma'am," she said suddenly. "But I needed the money and…"

"Nobody is judging you, Diana," I told her. "We've all come via very different paths."

"Oh, honey, don't take on so," said Sandra, getting up and putting her arms around Diana. "Some people might even call it a noble profession."

"It's certainly the oldest profession," quipped Connie.

"Thank you, Sandra," said Diana, gratefully accepting her embrace.

"But how did you end up in the Sirens?" Shelly asked her.

"I am very good with numbers. I can do arithmetic in my head. I used to keep the books for a friend. Then one day these two gentlemen turned up. They said they'd heard about my skill and thought I might make a good navigator."

I didn't ask how on earth the Marx Brothers had come by that piece of information.

"Right," I said. "So, it looks like we've got all the pieces of the jigsaw. Now we just have to put them all together."

"Laxington won't know what's hit him," said Pamela with a chuckle.

"Not if we do it right," I said.

We set to with a will in order to devise a plan.

In the end, I decided that I had to take the scheme to James. He needed to be kept informed. We were in his room together. He listened quietly while I outlined what we intended to do.

"And the two spies have agreed to this, have they?" he asked me.

"They will do so, yes," I said confidently.

"And you suppose that I'm going to sanction this … underhanded scheme?"

I stuck my chin out and looked him in the eye. "I don't care if you sanction it or not," I informed him. "I'm going to save the Sirens in spite of you, if I have to."

In response, James threw back his head and roared with laughter. "You know, you are everything I want in a woman and in a Flight Leader," he said. "Feisty, determined, persistent, independent…"

"Insubordinate?" I ventured.

"That too."

"Unmanageable?"

"Absolutely…"

"So, you agree with the plan?"

"I doubt I could stop you even if I didn't," he said.

"That's the right answer," I told him.

CHAPTER THIRTEEN

Laxington had spent the day touring the facilities and poking his nose into every part of the squadron. However, apparently he wasn't finished and would be staying at least one more night, Sally informed us. This was all to the good, since we needed to put our plan into action. Everyone had been cooperative at James's request, though most of the Sirens loathed Laxington.

As luck would have it, Laxington liked to have a drink or two, so he made his way down to the house bar in order to indulge in his favourite tipple. Sally had already told us about this habit, so we were prepared.

It gave us the perfect opportunity to act. Sandra was to lure Laxington up to her room, which had been rigged with concealed microphones. When called for, Sally would bring the drink for Laxington laced with the Marx Brothers' special potion. Once he had taken it, the spies would act. After the photographs had been taken and when he was awake again, Sandra would introduce Laxington to Diana. The Marx Brothers would record every word of his encounters with Sandra and Diana.

All that remained was the question of whether Laxington would take the bait. That was up to Sandra, and I was pretty confident in her ability to play her part.

Our group had seated itself in the bar, not far from where Laxington was drinking a beer on his own. Such was his unpopularity that nobody wanted to be in his company. He appeared to be somewhat oblivious to this fact, and I thought that his lack of awareness would work in our favour.

Sandra had made a special effort for the occasion. She was wearing her uniform, but her hair was shining, and she had paid particular attention to her makeup.

"When you've got a bee to catch, you've got to make the honey extra inviting," she said when she came to show us before we went downstairs.

"You've certainly done *that*," said Connie with admiration.

"I've learned a thing or two," said Sandra. "Red lipstick, for example, is guaranteed to get your man."

I filed this piece of information away for the future reference. Sandra was also wearing red nail polish to match the lipstick. WAAF regulations didn't permit nail polish while on duty. However, I was certain that James would turn a blind eye to it, and arguably Sandra wouldn't be officially on duty during 'Operation Honeypot', as we'd decided to call it.

Sandra had not joined us for a drink; instead, she was determined to make an entrance. That she most certainly did. She arrived at the bar looking like a million dollars. Laxington, who was about to take a swig of his beer, almost choked. His eyes started out of his head as Sandra walked across the room towards him with a dazzling smile on her face.

I had placed myself where I could get a full view of what went on between Sandra and Laxington. We were also within earshot, and Sandra had one of those voices which carried.

She stopped beside Laxington's table and put one perfectly polished hand on the surface. She leaned in slightly towards him.

"Air Commodore, it seems you are all on your lonesome here," she said, accentuating her Southern drawl.

Laxington coughed. "Well, you know," he said, "I'm just having a quiet drink. Busy day and all that."

"You look like you could use some company, sir. Do you mind if I join you?" She smiled and fluttered her eyelashes at him provocatively.

Laxington hesitated, and I wondered if our ruse was going to fail at the first hurdle. However, just as we'd hoped, he gestured to the seat opposite him.

"Why not? I'd be glad of it, Section Officer…?"

"Sandra Brown, sir, but you can call me Sandra," she said, sliding into the seat.

"Boarding party now in position, target in sight," murmured Shelly with a grin.

In short order, Laxington pompously snapped his fingers at the barman, who came over and took an order for drinks.

"I'll take a whisky and ice," said Sandra.

"I'll have the same, thanks," Laxington said. After the barman had left, he continued, "Whisky — that's a man's drink. I'm impressed."

"Oh, you know," said Sandra, at her smoothest, "I just love the way that golden liquid fire eases its way on down, don't you?"

"Ahem, yes, yes indeed," said Laxington. "Right, well now, did I tell you about the time I was in charge of a squadron of Tiger Moths?"

"No, but please, I'm all ears. It sounds so exciting…"

For the most part, the conversation was one-sided. Sandra prompted Laxington to become more and more boastful about his exploits in the Air Force, seemingly in awe of everything he said.

The evening wore on and the drinks flowed, although I noticed that Sandra was pacing herself. She had inched around to Laxington's side of the table and sat tight against him, with her arm around his shoulders. She had also started calling him "Laxie", which he didn't seem to mind.

"Don't you think this is so much cosier, Laxie?" she cooed.

"Well, yes … ahem … indeed."

"Good grief," said Pamela when we heard her use this pet name for the third time.

"Rather her than me," said Maria.

"She's doing it for us," said Connie. "Don't knock it."

Meanwhile, Sandra was regaling Laxington with stories of various dignitaries she had come into contact with. It seemed she had moved in high circles.

"So, you know, I said to the Ambassador, is that your wife or your mistress over there?"

"Oh, I would have loved to have seen his face," said Laxington, doubling up with mirth. He was laughing uproariously at practically everything she said.

I glanced at my watch; it was starting to get late, and the bar would be closing soon.

"It's almost time for Operation Honeypot to begin the attack phase," I said to the others.

"Thank goodness for that," said Pamela. "I don't think I can stomach much more of this."

"Shh," whispered Maria, putting a finger to her lips. Sandra was making her move.

"So, Laxie, why don't we take this somewhere a little more private?" she said.

"Well, I, er, I'm not really sure," said Laxington, looking slightly unnerved.

Were things going to fail at the last, I wondered? However, Sandra was nothing if not persistent.

"Oh, come on, Laxie, you're not going to disappoint me, are you?" she said, trailing one red nail lightly down his cheek.

"Well … I…" he said, suddenly tugging his collar as if it had become too tight.

Sandra dropped her voice and added a seductive husk to it. "Laxie, my darling, you know you want to … and you know I want you to … hmm? And what Sandra wants, darling … Sandra gets…"

Sandra was in full flow. I couldn't for the life of me imagine how he or anyone would be able to resist her.

Laxington came to a sudden decision. "All right, Sandra," he said. "Upstairs it is. Lead on, Macduff, as they say."

Laxington stood up. He seemed a little unsteady on his feet, but he let Sandra slip her hand into his and lead him out of the bar. As soon as they had gone, I sprang into action.

"I'm going to take up my post with the Marx Brothers," I said to the others. "I'll see you all in the War Room later, and I'll give you a full account, I promise." I hurried from the bar.

The room where Sandra had taken Laxington wasn't too far from his own. The Marx Brothers had already fitted it out with the requisite microphones and were stationed in the room next door. As I passed the door of the room where Sandra and Laxington were ensconced, I saw Sally waiting close by. She was holding a tray on which there were two glasses of liquid.

"I've got the potion ready for when Sandra needs it," she said to me.

"Good," I said. "When you've done that, you can come next door."

She nodded. I saw no reason why she shouldn't be party to the downfall of a boss whom she despised so much.

I slipped into the room where the Marx Brothers were listening intently on sets of headphones. Sitting apart from the Marx Brothers was Diana, wearing a dressing gown. She smiled at me, and I smiled back. She was waiting for her cue. Harpo passed another pair of headphones to me. I put them on, and I could hear Sandra and Laxington as clear as day.

"Oh my," said Laxington. "You're certainly all woman."

"Of course, and you'll get to find out exactly how much, darling."

He sounded like nothing so much as an eager puppy waiting for a treat. Sandra was playing him like a virtuoso on a violin.

"Let's get these clothes off you, and then I'll get Sally to bring us a nightcap."

"Do we really need one? I mean, I've had rather a lot to drink already."

There were sounds akin to the rustling of clothing while Sandra made appreciative murmurs. Laxington was taking the bait, hook, line and sinker.

"Come on, Laxie, a nightcap will do you good, set us both up."

"Well, all right, if you say so."

Sandra went over to the door, which opened briefly and closed. Then there was the clink of glasses. Having performed that vital office, Sally came into our room. I beckoned her over to me. I took my headphones off so that we could both lean into them and listen together.

"Here you are, Laxie, drink up," Sandra was saying.

"What is this?" he asked.

"It's a Martini, darling. I am American, after all."

"Oh, well, all right. What about you?"

"Oh, mine's right here. What is it you say in England? Down the hatch."

"Yes, indeed, down the hatch."

I turned to Sally. "She knows which the right one is, doesn't she?" I asked her.

"His is the one with the olive in it," she told me.

It went quiet in the room next door for a moment, I assumed while they were drinking. Then Laxington spoke, but he was slurring his words.

"I don't feel well, Sandra, not sure what's happening but I ... oh dear ... maybe it was that olive..."

Then there was silence.

"Laxie? Laxie, are you all right?" said Sandra after a moment, presumably checking if he was really asleep. A moment later, she said, "He's out. You can come in."

"That's our cue," said Harpo.

In short order, we were all in the room where Laxington was lying out cold on the bed in his underwear. Sandra was also down to her underwear, but Harpo and Chico took no notice and instead bustled around, setting up lights and getting the camera ready. I assumed that this was all grist to the mill for them. I was pretty sure it wasn't the first time they'd done something like this, judging by the speed at which they worked.

"All right," said Chico, once everything was ready. "Let's get to it, no time to lose."

Diana divested herself of her dressing gown. She was wearing a rather fetching corset.

With a little direction from Harpo and Chico, Diana and Sandra arranged themselves and Laxington in various compromising positions. Sally and I watched from the sidelines. The Marx Brothers were certainly adept with the photography and knew exactly what they were doing. They managed to pose Laxington in such a way that you couldn't tell he was asleep. After they had shot several rolls of film, they decided they had got enough material.

"What happens now?" I asked as they packed up their gear.

Harpo checked his watch. "Now we wait. Laxington should come round soon enough and if not, we have something you can inject him with to hasten it."

"After which, the ladies will begin the second act," said Chico with a flourish.

Act two would involve Laxington being coaxed into revealing his relationship with Diana, so that it could be recorded.

We returned to the other room, leaving Sandra and Diana waiting for Laxington to wake up. The Marx Brothers lit up cigarettes and smoked them with evident satisfaction. They hadn't smoked while doing the photography, since they didn't want to leave any trace of themselves in the room.

"A good evening's work so far," said Harpo.

"Absolutely," said Chico.

"Will it be long, do you think?" I asked them.

Harpo checked his watch again. "Shouldn't be," he said. "We're pretty good at the dosages these days."

I wondered exactly how many people they'd drugged in the past. It made me realise that as benign as they might appear, they were certainly ruthless. I wouldn't have liked to find myself on the wrong side of them.

After a while, the sound of Laxington groaning emanated suddenly from the headphones. The four of us sat listening intently to the goings-on next door.

"Oh God, what happened?" said Laxington, sounding a bit groggy.

"You had a little too much to drink, Laxie, but we really had a lot of fun, don't you remember?" said Sandra.

"No, I don't. It's all gone blank. Are you sure?" he replied, sounding doubtful.

"Oh yes, Laxie, you were everything a woman could desire, I promise you that," said Sandra.

Sally suppressed a chuckle on hearing this. Sandra was really laying it on thick.

"Well damn," said Laxington. "It's a shame I can't recall it..."

"But *I* will always remember it, Laxie darling —"

Evidently Laxington suddenly noticed Diana, as he interrupted Sandra.

"What on earth is she doing here?" he said.

"Don't you remember me, Laxington darling?" said Diana softly.

"What? Should I?"

"Oh, I'm so disappointed after all those times we spent together," said Diana.

Laxington was evidently struggling with the recollection, but after a moment he exclaimed, "Good lord, is it Diana? I hardly recognised you."

"But I recognised *you*," she said. "All those lovely times, darling. Remember how you liked me to tie you up, call you names, hmm?"

She didn't waste any time in getting to the nub of it; it was vital to get this on tape.

"Ah, yes, well, of course. Those were different times," he said hastily.

"But you loved it, didn't you, darling? Tell me that you loved me being ever so strict with my naughty Laxington?" Diana crooned.

Sally was trying not to laugh as we listened.

"I did, of course, but there's no need to dwell on the past," Laxington said, desperately trying to change the subject.

But Diana wasn't finished. She needed to punch the point home that it wasn't a one-off. "So many nights we spent together, misbehaving. Over several months too. We had such good times, didn't we?"

"Yes, all right, they *were* good times. I enjoyed them immensely, but now…" Laxington hesitated.

"Don't worry, darling, your secret is safe," said Diana. "I won't tell anyone that you hired me as an escort companion, I promise."

There it was — the vital incriminating information. Laxington sighed. It was evident he wasn't in the least comfortable discussing it.

"Yes, that's very good of you. Not the sort of thing I want made public, and I'm sure Sandra here doesn't need to know about my little peccadillos."

"Oh, but I do, Laxie darling," said Sandra. "Diana told me all about it while you were asleep."

"She did what?" said Laxington, sounding alarmed.

"Oh yes, Laxie, and we thought you might like a repeat performance with both of us. Diana has brought some nice strong rope just like she used to use…" Sandra continued relentlessly.

"Yes, well, perhaps another time. I don't think…" began Laxington, backpedalling as rapidly as he could.

Sandra wasn't to be deterred. "Oh, Laxie, and here I was thinking you were all ready for round two."

There was the sound of frantic rustling as Laxington sought to make his escape.

"Laxie, where are you going? Aren't you going to stay with us?" asked Sandra.

Laxington sounded as if he was on the verge of sheer panic. "I've just remembered, I've urgent things to do … some paperwork…"

"But Laxie, darling…" Sandra said in a voice laced with disappointment.

Laxington had evidently had enough. "It's been very nice, ladies, but I've got to go."

Rapid steps headed over to the door.

"Laxie, come back," pleaded Sandra.

"Sorry, duty calls … and, of course, you'll keep all this to yourselves, won't you?" said Laxington quickly, before opening the door and shutting it rather firmly behind him.

Moments later, Sandra and Diana went off into peals of laughter. Harpo switched off the recording machine.

We all went into the other room, to find that Sandra and Diana had collapsed on the bed with mirth.

"Oh, Boss, you should have seen his face," said Sandra to me.

"It was a picture," added Diana.

"I've never seen a man run quite so fast," Sandra said, still laughing.

"Well done," said Harpo. "We've got everything we need. You can stand down, but if ever you fancy a spell at MI6, we'd be happy to have you."

"Come on," I said to Sandra and Diana. "Let's go back to the War Room."

Sandra threw on a robe and picked up her discarded uniform.

"Jolly good," said Chico. "We'll tidy things up here, get those photographs printed pronto, and then we'll go in for the kill."

"Not literally, of course," quipped Harpo.

"No indeed," said Chico.

We took our leave of the Marx Brothers, then, laughing and joking, we wended our way to my room, where the rest of the gang would be eagerly waiting to hear what had happened. I decided to let Sandra tell them, since I was sure she would do it well.

Later that night, I slipped into James's room and into his bed. He automatically pulled me into an embrace.

"And what have you been up to?" he said. "As if I didn't know."

"The deed is almost done," I said. "At least, the hard part is over. Now it's up to the Marx Brothers to convince Laxington to cease and desist."

James chuckled. "I've no doubt they'll be able to do that, but anyway, go on … tell me what happened."

"Are you sure you want to know?" I asked doubtfully.

"Yes, of course."

"You might be rather shocked," I told him.

"I think you'll find I'm less shockable than you imagine," he replied. "Come on, tell me the whole and don't spare the details." He sat up and lay back against the headboard.

"Well, you should have seen Sandra. She could easily take to the stage with her acting skills…" I began, and then summarised all that had followed.

After James had heard it all, he smiled. "You Sirens never cease to amaze me. Your resourcefulness knows no bounds."

"Well, of course," I said, leaning closer. "That's because we're women."

The next day went by rather quickly. Laxington was not seen all day and according to Sally had taken to his bed with some sort of malaise. I thought perhaps he might be apprehensive about running into Sandra or Diana. However, he didn't seem to be the kind of man who worried much about things like that.

Shortly after dinner, Judy came to find me. She took me up to the Marx Brothers' interrogation room. Inside, I found them waiting.

"We've got the photographs," said Harpo.

"So now all we need is Laxington," said Chico.

"He'll be with us shortly," said Harpo. "So perhaps you'd like to go into the secret room."

I readily agreed, since I didn't want to miss this for the world. The room was accessed through a secret panel in the wainscoting and up some stairs. Through a grille, I could see everything that went on.

Not long after I had settled down to wait in the chair provided, Laxington arrived, ushered into the room by Judy. He looked somewhat irritated as she closed the door behind him.

"Air Commodore," said Harpo. "Nice to see you."

"And who might you be?" Laxington demanded, advancing into the room.

"Who we are is not your concern," said Chico.

"I think it's very much my concern," Laxington shot back. "I've been dragged from my sickbed for this meeting, and I demand to know what it's all about."

Laxington's style was all bluster. I assumed he'd got where he was partly by being exceptionally rude and overbearing. I knew the Marx Brothers would cut him down to size.

"We're from MI6. That's all you need to know," said Harpo.

"Oh, I see," said Laxington, slightly amending his attitude.

"Take a seat, Air Commodore," said Chico, indicating a chair at the table.

Laxington sat down while the two spies lit up cigarettes and smoked them without saying a word. Being familiar with this behaviour, I wasn't surprised, but Laxington looked a little unnerved.

"So," he said after a few minutes had passed, "what is this about?"

"All in good time," said Chico, blowing out smoke and watching it curl up towards the ceiling.

"Now, look here —" Laxington began.

"No, you look here," said Harpo, cutting in. "In fact, take a look at these and tell me if you recognise anyone in them."

He picked up an envelope that was lying on the table and pulled out several photographs. Harpo laid them out one by one in front of Laxington. He stared at them for a few seconds before exploding.

"This is outrageous!" he thundered.

"Isn't it?" said Harpo, unmoved.

"One might even say indecent," said Chico laconically.

I suppressed a chuckle. The photographs were, as I expected, of Laxington in various compromising positions with Sandra and Diana.

"How did you obtain these photographs?" Laxington demanded. "I insist on you telling me."

"Well, since you insist… We took them," said Harpo.

"What!" said Laxington, flabbergasted.

"Yes," Harpo continued. "We took them. They're rather good, don't you think?"

"How dare you invade my privacy in this fashion! I demand an explanation!" said Laxington, angrily banging his fist on the table.

"We've also got a recording," said Harpo, ignoring this. "It contains an interesting conversation between you and Diana, a former escort companion, in which you clearly admit to recalling many occasions where you and she engaged in, shall we say, some rather interesting practices involving rope, among other things."

"Would you like to hear it?" asked Chico.

"No, I bloody well would not," said Laxington, infuriated.

"Pity," said Chico. "We thought it was rather entertaining. I'm sure your superiors would be most interested in it."

"And of course these photographs," said Harpo.

On hearing this, Laxington suddenly deflated. "What do you want?" he asked with heavy resignation.

"We want you to leave the Sirens alone, old chum, that's about the size of it," said Chico.

"And if I refuse?"

"Well, think of your illustrious career and all that you've built. Wouldn't like that to be for nothing, would you?" said Harpo.

"Are you blackmailing me?" said Laxington, as if he'd only just worked it out.

"Let's just say we're encouraging you to take a more considered approach towards this unit," said Chico with a smile.

"I'll have you know I'm very highly regarded in certain circles," said Laxington pompously. "I doubt something like this will particularly faze them at all."

He was attempting to call their bluff, but the Marx Brothers were made of sterner stuff. He also had no idea of the elevated circles they undoubtedly moved in.

"Do you know the story of Ernst Röhm?" said Harpo.

"Not particularly, no, but no doubt you are going to tell me," said Laxington. It was plain that he had taken the Marx Brothers in extreme dislike.

"Röhm was one of Hitler's right-hand men who helped him to seize power. A trusted confidant, who thought he was bulletproof due to his position. Hitler tolerated his sexual preferences because he was useful. But when he was no longer useful, he was arrested on trumped-up charges. He was given a Luger by the SS and told to use it. He didn't take up their offer, so they shot him dead anyway," said Harpo.

Laxington paled. "What are you suggesting?"

"We're suggesting that you're in over your head, and that the protection you think you have from your colleagues might not be enough, were your secrets to become known. So why not just let it go, old man?"

"Are you threatening me?" said Laxington, who seemed determined not to completely lose face.

"It's not just a threat," said Chico with a hint of steel in his voice. "We don't make threats we're not prepared to carry out."

Laxington gave a rather deep sigh. He knew that he'd been thoroughly outplayed.

"Fine. So what do you want me to do?"

Harpo tapped his ash into the ashtray and smiled. "We want you to walk away and leave the Sirens alone."

"And if I do?"

"We'll leave you alone."

"All right, fine," said Laxington, getting up.

"Not so fast, Air Commodore," said Chico, motioning for him to sit.

"What now?"

"Just this," said Harpo. "You've made rather a nuisance of yourself while you've been here, upset a lot of people, and now you're going to make amends."

"And how exactly am I supposed to do that?"

Chico picked up the thread. "You're going to attend a flying display before you go, arranged by the Sirens. Afterwards, you are going to tell them that you've had a change of heart. Now that you've seen what a splendid job they're doing, you have not only revised your opinion, but you are going to write a report to your superiors to that effect. You will tell them how much you admire this unit and the women who are part of it."

"Anything else?" asked Laxington acidly.

"You will write a report praising the Sirens, and furthermore you will give us your assurance that you won't arrange any more conflicting missions with our targets," added Harpo.

"You must think you have a lot of support, the way you're carrying on," said Laxington.

"We do," said Chico. "Far higher up than you can imagine."

"As high as it goes," said Harpo.

Laxington was finally defeated. "All right, I will do as you say, but if I do, what happens to the photographs and recordings?"

"They'll be held in safekeeping at MI6 to ensure that you keep to your agreement," said Harpo.

"There's no winning with you bloody spies, is there?" said Laxington bitterly.

"Take our advice, old chum, and don't start something you can't finish," said Harpo.

The two of them smiled at him benignly, which only served to infuriate him all over again. However, Laxington thought better of prolonging his agony. He stood up and saluted rather stiffly.

"I'll see you at the flying display then, I suppose," he said.

"Indubitably," said Harpo.

"Absolutely," said Chico.

Laxington turned on his heel and marched out of the room. He shut the door behind him with unnecessary violence. When he had gone, I left my hiding place and went back into the room.

"Flight Officer, I trust that went to your satisfaction," said Harpo.

"Oh, it did," I said. "I enjoyed it immensely."

"He didn't seem entirely happy," said Chico. "But you can't please everybody."

I laughed at his deadpan delivery.

"Anyway," said Harpo, "all's well that ends well."

"I'd better go and see the others," I said. "Since I've now got a flying display to arrange."

I took my leave and practically skipped back to my room. The outcome was far better than I had expected. As long as Laxington kept his promise, the future of the Sirens was hopefully safe.

CHAPTER FOURTEEN

The following morning, James held a briefing. I sat at the front with the usual gang as he took to the podium along with Henry, Gloria and the Marx Brothers. I was surprised not to see Laxington, but perhaps he'd thought better of facing us all before the flying display. The Marx Brothers had made him aware of the animosity he had already engendered.

"At ease," said James, stepping forward. "This afternoon the entire squadron will hold a flying display for the Air Commodore."

There was a collective groan from everyone in the room, with the exception of those who were in on the secret.

"All right, all right," said James, smiling and holding up his hands. "Regardless of what has been said, we are going to show the Air Commodore what we are made of. We're going to show him that this is a professional outfit as good as any in the RAF."

"Damn right about that!" Cynthia piped up.

Her pronouncement was met with murmurs of agreement.

"Never let it be said," James continued, "that the Sirens kowtow to anybody. Today is your day to shine, so make it count."

Naturally, knowing what he knew, he was able to exude more confidence than the others would be feeling. However, the subterfuge had to be complete. Laxington had to be handed a reason for changing his mind. The flying display was that reason.

"Now, I'm going to ask Flight Officer Nightingale — who will be leading the display — to give you all the details."

He smiled at me as I walked up to the front.

"All right, Sirens," I said, "this is what we are going to do…"

Having covered the order of events, the briefing broke up. I had decided to keep it simple, flying in close formation, low-level attack runs and so forth. Laxington would be taken out to the nearby target range, where we would strafe some targets and drop some ordnance just for show.

The morning passed quite quickly, as we liaised with the ground crew and maintenance crew to ensure all was right and tight with the Mosquitos. The firing range had to be informed at quite short notice. However, after lunch we headed out to the airfield in the trucks.

"Do you think Laxington will keep his word?" Maria asked me as we trundled down the familiar track.

"Oh, he'll keep it," I said. "Absolutely."

"Then let's make it a good one," said Jennifer.

"Of course," said Connie, handing her a cigarette. "We're the Sirens."

In short order we were once more strapped in and ready to go. I fired up the engines and when everyone was ready, I spoke to Control.

"Bluebird Leader requesting clearance," I said.

"Roger, Bluebird Leader, you're clear."

"Bluebirds, let's go."

I eased the Mosquito out from the standing and headed down towards the runway. Once there, I throttled up and we were quickly airborne. Shortly we were joined by the others.

"Bluebirds, close formation," I said.

Maria gave us the bearing. We would fly in the opposite direction to the range and then come back in towards it.

"Bluebird Leader, the Air Commodore is in position," said Control over the radio.

"Roger," I said. "All right, Bluebirds, let's show him what we've got."

We approached the range, and some way off from the target I could see a small group of figures, which would be James, Laxington and the others.

It was unusual for us to be flying in formation with eighteen planes. It was quite a feat and a testament to the hours of practice we had put in. I was able to wheel the flight around the range with some precision. Having done that, we moved on to the next part of the display.

"Low-level flying, Bluebirds," I said.

We banked around and I took the kite as low as I dared, along with the rest of the flight. Then we flew several close passes over the range, almost cutting the daisies.

"Let's hope Laxington is suitably impressed," said Maria dryly after our third pass.

"Well, let's show him some combat, shall we? Bluebirds, attack run," I said, banking around again.

We split into three groups of six and flew low-level strafing runs against the hastily put up plane cutouts. By the end of it they were shredded, and I was pleased with how things had gone so far.

"All right, Bluebirds, bombing run," I said.

I'd decided to run groups of three planes dropping ordnance on a large X painted on the ground. The groups had to time it so that they would not fly into the blast from the previous one.

I led the first group, dropped the bombs and circled around to watch the others. This was the only part I was concerned about. It had to go perfectly.

Six groups went one after the other, blast after blast filling the air with smoke. Thankfully it went without a hitch.

"Well," said Maria, "that's that. Let's hope he's suitably impressed."

"He's duty-bound to say he is, regardless," I said, laughing.

"I know, but I still actually want him to be impressed," she said.

The flight reformed and we passed over Laxington's group, dipping our wings, then we returned to base. A thought was forming in my mind as to how I might impress the Air Commodore further.

We landed and taxied back to our standings. James and the others were waiting for us. Maria and I approached and saluted smartly.

"This is our Flight Leader, Flight Officer Nightingale and her navigator ASO Preston, sir," said James by way of introduction to Laxington.

"Ah, yes, jolly good," said Laxington, beaming at me. "Excellent display up there."

"Thank you, sir." I hesitated and then took the plunge. "I was wondering, would you like a quick spin in a Mosquito?"

Maria and James shot me an enquiring look, but I kept my face neutral.

"Well," said Laxington, looking doubtful. "I'm not sure that…"

He stopped abruptly, having spied Sandra and Diana approaching our group along with the other Sirens. He took on a somewhat hunted look and appeared to rapidly change his mind, much to my amusement. I doubted he wanted to come into contact with them again.

"Actually, yes, it's a splendid idea. I'll get to see your skills first-hand," he said. "Lead on, Flight Officer, lead on."

"This way, sir," I said, indicating my Mosquito.

"Excellent," he said, hurrying towards the plane.

We climbed aboard and I strapped back in, with Laxington in the navigator's seat.

"Ready, sir?" I asked him.

"Yes, indeed. It's been a while since I took a spin in a plane, so I'm rather looking forward to it," he replied.

I fired up the engines, got clearance from the Tower and taxied the Mosquito back to the bottom of the runway. I executed a take-off in textbook fashion, and we were soon airborne.

"I say," he said enthusiastically as we banked around. "This is rather good."

"Have you been in a Mosquito before, sir?" I asked him.

"Not for some time," he replied. "I had forgotten what excellent planes they are."

"Shall I put her through her paces?"

"Well, if you like," he said, a little doubtfully.

I was sure that Laxington was expecting a quick ride and then back to base. I had other ideas. I opened up the throttle and proceeded to execute a series of tight banking turns.

"She manoeuvres well, doesn't she?" said Laxington, starting to look a little pale.

However, I wasn't disposed to let him off quite so easily. "I'll show you some low flying, shall I?" I said.

Before he could answer, I took the Mosquito down low. I opened up the throttle and the ground flashed by at a tremendous pace.

"I say, this is rather fast," said Laxington nervously.

"Yes, it's the speed we usually go," I said airily.

"Is it?" said Laxington, not looking at all comfortable with the proceedings.

"Yes, of course."

"Watch out for that house!" Laxington suddenly shouted, aware that we were approaching a farm building at speed.

"Seen it, sir…"

"Those telegraphs lines are awfully close."

"Not to worry, sir."

"There's a bank of trees just up ahead, in case you hadn't… Oh my God, that was rather too close," he gasped as we almost clipped the treetops.

I desperately tried not to laugh. Poor Laxington would not forget this flight in a hurry.

"Of course, it's a little more exciting when we do this at night," I informed him.

"At night? Oh, yes, of course. Well, I don't think I need to see *that*," he said. "And if you don't mind, I'd be obliged if we could go back."

"Of course, sir," I said, turning suddenly while still very low to the ground.

"Christ! Can you please slow down?" exclaimed Laxington.

Feeling that he'd definitely had enough, I took the Mosquito back up to a decent height and eased up on the throttle. Laxington retrieved a handkerchief from his pocket and mopped his brow.

"Are you all right, sir?" I asked him solicitously.

"What? Oh, yes, it's just a trifle warm in here."

"We'll soon be back on solid ground, sir," I said.

"Yes, well, good show, excellent flying skills," he said, putting on a brave face.

"Thank you, sir," I said, giving him my sweetest smile.

Once we had landed, I walked with Laxington to where James was waiting. James raised an eyebrow at me briefly, suppressing a smile.

"How was that, sir?" he asked Laxington.

"Most invigorating, yes ... excellent piloting skills from Flight Officer ... Nightingale, is it?"

"Yes, sir," I said. "And thank you."

"Don't mention it," he said, looking very much as if he'd like to put the entire episode firmly behind him. However, he had one more promise to keep.

"Would you like to see anything else, sir?" James asked.

"No thank you, Wing Commander. I've seen enough. If you would be so good as to assemble everyone in your briefing room, I've got something to say before I depart, which I will be doing without delay," Laxington said, starting to regain his composure.

"This way, sir," said Gloria, indicating the staff car.

"Back to Hawberry, everyone," said James.

He hung back as the Sirens made their way to the trucks and spoke to me quietly.

"What exactly were you playing at, taking him up for a spin?" he asked me.

"I was just showing the Air Commodore what good pilots we are," I said innocently.

"Is that what you call it?"

"That and perhaps a little bit of payback..."

"You are a dangerous woman," he said with a smile.

"You've only just discovered it?" I shot back.

James laughed and made his way to the waiting vehicle, while I went to join the others in the truck.

Not long after, we were once more assembled in the briefing room, where Laxington stood on the podium along with James, Henry, Gloria and the Marx Brothers. He smiled somewhat benignly at us.

"Well," Laxington began, "that was quite a show you all put on, quite a show indeed."

This pronouncement was met with stony silence. No doubt the rest of the squadron would be expecting a repetition of his earlier speech about shutting us down.

"I've inspected your facilities thoroughly, and I'm happy to say —" he paused, as if finding it somewhat difficult to get the words out — "I'm happy to say that this is one of the finest units I have come across in the RAF."

I noticed some rather surprised expressions as he said this.

"Indeed, I misspoke the last time I was on this podium. I put this down entirely to not being properly briefed before coming here."

James's face was a picture of scepticism. Laxington wasn't going to take the blame; he was going to firmly place it somewhere else.

"It is obvious to me that you are as capable in combat as any all-male squadrons. This is a fact I will certainly be endorsing in my report."

To say the audience was stunned would be an understatement. The complete volte-face that Laxington had pulled off was nothing short of miraculous to those not in the know.

"Yes, I just want to say what a great job you are all doing. I have great admiration for you, putting your lives on the line. Well done, Sirens. I salute you!"

So saying, he stood to attention and snapped a very smart salute. We all, naturally, did the same. Once we were seated again, he finished up his speech.

"Anyway, it's time for me to say *au revoir*. It's unlikely I will be back, as I have many pressing duties to attend to at Bomber

Command. However, rest assured I will be carrying the torch for you all from now on."

Suddenly, Sandra stood up and shouted, "Three cheers for the Air Commodore! Hip hip hooray…"

The room erupted into thunderous cheers while Laxington stood smiling smugly. I had no doubt that had he not been coerced, he would have gone out of his way to try to engineer the demise of the Sirens. I was also pretty sure he'd never set foot in Hawberry Hall again, for which I was truly thankful.

Once the cheers subsided, Laxington took his leave and departed with his adjutant, Sally, close behind. She shot me a glance and I gave her a brief nod. I would see what I could do to get her into the Sirens; it was only fair, considering the service she had done for us.

"I'm not sorry to see him go," said Shelly once Laxington had gone.

"No, thank goodness we can put that behind us," said Patricia.

"Thanks in no small part to Sandra," I said. "And, of course, Diana."

The two of them had joined us. Diana had *de facto* now become a member of our little band.

"Perhaps we can get back to business as usual," said Maria. "I wonder what that will be."

"Missions and then more missions," said Shelly, to general laughter.

"What about that dance, Boss?" said Sandra, looking me straight in the eye.

"Oh, well, all right. I promise I will talk to James," I said.

I couldn't put it off any longer and besides, it might just be the tonic we all needed. Laxington's appearance had cast something of a damper on the whole base, in spite of him recanting at the end.

I went directly to James's office only to find him ensconced with Gloria and Henry. He smiled as soon as he saw me.

"Anna," he said. "What can we do for you?"

"Am I interrupting anything?" I asked, noting that they were sitting in the armchairs and drinking tea.

"No, no," said James. "We were just celebrating the departure of the Air Commodore. It would have been something a little stronger, but we're all on duty."

Gloria raised her teacup in salute to what was an auspicious moment.

"Here's to Air Commodore Laxington," she said. "May he never return to Hawberry."

"Amen to that," said Henry.

Laxington had obviously been something of a thorn in their side too.

"I just wanted to ask you a question, sir," I said.

"Have a seat. Would you like some tea?" James offered.

I accepted graciously and sat down on the sofa.

James poured a cup of tea, added milk and one sugar, and then handed it to me. There were curious glances from the other two, since he hadn't asked me how I liked my tea, but they didn't say anything.

"How can we help?" said James when I had taken a sip of the brew.

"I've been asked about the possibility of holding a dance," I said tentatively.

"A dance?" said James.

"Yes, for everyone in the Sirens, some entertainment … a celebration," I continued.

"I see, but I don't see how we —" James began.

"I think it's a splendid idea," Gloria cut in. "Just the lift everyone needs. We've had some trying times recently. Aborted missions, the visit from the Air Commodore and so forth."

"Sounds good to me," said Henry.

I smiled at James a little triumphantly. However, it seemed his hesitancy was not about the dance itself.

"I can certainly see the merit of it," said James. "It's just that for a dance we need a band and, well, how are we going to find a band who will preserve the secrecy of the Sirens?"

Now he pointed it out, this did seem to be a conundrum. If we got in outsiders or even a band from within the RAF, it would perforce break our protocols.

"Is a band strictly necessary?" Henry wondered. "Couldn't we just play records?"

"No, no, of course we need a band," said James, more enthusiastically. "You can't have a dance without live music. I just don't see how it can be accomplished. We don't have a band in the Sirens — it's not part of our brief."

Gloria, who had been smiling all through this, suddenly said, "Well, that's where you're wrong."

"Pardon?" said James, looking puzzled.

"We have a band of sorts. The ground crew and mechanics practise in their spare time — quite a few of them play instruments," Gloria continued.

"And how come I've never heard of this before?" James demanded.

"There's quite a few things which go on here, under the radar, so to speak," said Gloria.

"So it seems," said James. I knew he liked to be kept informed about everything that went on at Hawberry.

I brought things back to the point. "So, is the problem solved? Can we have the dance?" I asked.

"It looks like you shall go to the ball after all, Cinderella," said James with a laugh.

"The girls will be pleased," I said. "Particularly Sandra, since it was her idea. She's been asking about it for ages."

"Perfect," said Gloria. "If she's so keen, we can put her in charge of the arrangements."

The matter was settled, and from then on what seemed like a small undertaking became a magnum opus under Sandra's aegis.

When I found the gang and informed Sandra, she let out a whoop.

"Woohoo! This is going to be the best dance ever, you'll see!" she said joyfully. "A real dance, American-style."

"God help us all," said Maria, but I could tell she was secretly pleased, as was the entire squadron when the dance was announced at the next briefing.

"Since there are no forthcoming missions in the immediate future, it's been decided that we'll hold the dance without delay," said James, amidst applause and cheers from the Sirens. "SO Sandra Brown is the dance coordinator and we're giving her a free hand. So, if you're asked to help, please do step up."

"Hooray for Sandra!" shouted Diana.

"And so saying, I will leave you in her capable hands," said James. "Sandra, the floor is yours."

"Now then," said Sandra, going up to the front of the room. "I'm going to need…"

Sandra commandeered people left and right to do her bidding. To my surprise, the entire thing took less than a week to put together.

The band — led by Victoria on the saxophone — practised for all it was worth in one of the hangars. Hawberry Hall's unused ballroom was dusted off and finally put to the use for which it was intended. Bedecked with decorations, it looked rather splendid. There was a buffet, a bar and of course the promised band — American-style, just as Sandra had promised.

For once we were allowed out of uniform, and we put on our glad rags. Dresses that had hung in closets ever since we'd arrived at Hawberry were washed and pressed. Everyone was done up to the nines.

The dance went off splendidly. James made a point of standing up with every Siren at least once. The big surprise of the night was when the band announced a guest singer.

"And now," said Victoria, "I'd like to invite up on stage someone who is going to set this joint jumping, as they say in the USA, which is apt since she is here all the way from America — the one and only Section Officer Sandra Brown!"

The hall erupted with cheers and whistles. Sandra stepped up to the mic and started to sing.

"That girl's got a set of pipes on her for sure," said Maria as we listened to Sandra's melodious tones.

"Wonders will never cease," said Patricia.

"Never mind all that. Let's dance," said Connie.

The dancefloor was constantly full. Women danced with men and women danced with women, too, since they outnumbered the men by a large margin. Thus, Jennifer and Connie dancing close together wasn't remarked upon by anyone.

The evening wore on and I finally managed to get on the dancefloor with James for a slow number. He was looking handsome in a dinner jacket and bow tie.

"You look beautiful," he said quietly as we danced. "Just like Cinderella."

I took the compliment and smiled. "Thank you. You look very dashing yourself."

He lowered his voice a little. "If only we didn't have to keep things secret," he said. He leant forward for a moment. "I could kiss you right now," he whispered in my ear.

"But you won't," I whispered back, smiling.

He sighed and I resisted the temptation to lay my head on his shoulder, wishing that things could be different. I didn't know how to overcome my scruples. I didn't know if I ever could.

CHAPTER FIFTEEN

A few days after the dance, James called me up to his office.

"Anna," he said, drawing me over to the sofa after we had embraced, "I've got another mission for you."

I had been expecting it, since the distraction of Laxington was now over. We could get back to business as usual. I was glad, because that was the job we'd trained to do.

"The target is the same airbase as last time," he told me.

I was somewhat surprised to hear this. "But I thought the RAF just bombed it?"

"Yes, they did, but it's a key target and the top brass want to keep Jerry on the backfoot, so to speak. So, if we hit them again, then we can negate some of the repairs they've been doing."

This made sense, so we went on to discuss the details.

"All right, so is it a three-plane mission as usual?"

James shook his head. "I think you should take six, just to be on the safe side. You'll do more damage that way."

I was happy to take six planes. It would make the job easier, in a way.

"Is it the usual — strafe and bomb?"

"Yes, exactly so."

"All right," I said.

"Who will you pick?"

I thought about it for a few moments before settling on some names. "I'll take Jenny and Shelly, Patricia and Connie, Molly and Eileen, Sandra and Lucy, and SO Dorothy Farmer and Diana."

"Not Susan and Pamela?" he asked.

"I don't think we need two radar planes," I said. "We'll make do with one."

"All right." He paused for a moment. "I notice you never take Linda on these smaller missions."

I sighed. "I don't trust her, James. Not after she tried to undermine my position as Flight Leader."

"Do you want me to get rid of her?" he said seriously. "I know Gloria doesn't put you two together for the same reason."

"No," I said. "She's a good pilot. I just don't want her on my team, unless it's the full squadron. Besides, she hasn't done anything else, not to my knowledge."

He let it drop. I didn't want my personal feelings, nor the fact that I had the CO's ear, to influence such decisions. That would be very unfair.

"That's settled then," said James. "I will announce the mission at the next briefing."

"All right."

He took my hand and held it tight. "Take care up there, Anna."

I smiled at him. "Are you worried about me, James?" I said, shooting him a teasing look.

"Yes, shouldn't I be?"

"You should, but I always do my best to come back, you know."

He was silent for a few moments. "You know," he said at length, "when I was flying sorties in the Battle of Britain, I always wondered about those pilots with wives or girlfriends. How they felt when their men were flying into combat day after day. Now I know."

"And how did the pilots feel, leaving their partners?" I asked him.

"Well, all their attention was on the sorties. I don't think they had time to think about it," he said.

"That's where we're different then, darling," I said. "Because you're never out of my mind, not for a minute."

"I'm rather glad you said so," he replied, pulling me into an embrace.

"And why is that?" I asked him lightly.

"Because it's the same for me."

Then there was nothing else to do but kiss him.

The night of the mission came around soon enough. At well past midnight, the five crews I had picked, plus myself and Maria, were on our way to the airfield.

"I hope that we're not going to have to abort this time," said Sandra.

"Third time lucky, maybe," said Shelly.

"It's going to be fine," said Connie. "I can feel it."

She tapped the ash off the end of her cigarette and handed it back to Jennifer.

Victoria was waiting, as usual, with the Mosquitos. She saluted as I came up to her.

"All right and tight, ma'am," she said. "Ready for the off."

"Thank you, Victoria," I said, returning the salute. "By the way, you play a pretty mean sax, if I may say so."

"Thank you," she replied. It was too dark to tell if she was blushing.

"Let's get to it," I said to the others.

In short order, Maria and I were in our Mosquito with the engines running. The others were also ready to go.

"Badger Leader requesting clearance," I said to Control.

"Badger Leader, you're clear," came the response.

"Badgers, let's get this done," I said, easing out of the standing and heading for the runway.

Shortly afterwards, we were airborne. I gave the command for low-level flying, while Maria gave us the bearing.

We took the same route as before, west of London and the Chilterns then down to Bournemouth before leaving the British coastline. It was a pleasant enough trip and soon we came upon a familiar sight.

"Stonehenge," said Maria, covering her usual role as the second pair of eyes.

"Got it," I said.

We were approaching the stones very low this time. I did an up-and-over before dropping down again.

"Those certainly are big stones," said Maria as they receded behind us.

"Well, now you've seen them close up," I said.

"I don't need to see them any closer," Maria replied. "Certainly not while flying in a Mosquito."

The time seemed to go by quite quickly. It was probably because we had flown the route already. Before too long we passed Bournemouth and headed out across the Channel.

The waves flashed by beneath us. The Channel was a little frothy, with plenty of white tops. I kept a little higher than I normally would due to the windy conditions. I didn't want any of us getting blown into the sea.

Then Maria called out the time to target.

"Ten minutes to the Circus Show," she said. Circus Show was the codename for the target.

"All right," I replied, easing off the safety on the guns. "Let's hope nobody is waiting for us this time."

"As my Aunty Ethel would say," Maria quipped, "it's going to be all right — I can feel it in my bones."

"I hope your Aunty Ethel is right then," I replied with a smile.

"She's dead."

"And you're telling me this now?"

We couldn't help laughing, but not for long. The shoreline was approaching and beyond that was a short hop to the airbase.

"Circus Show in five," said Maria.

I readied myself for the attack and opened up the bomb doors.

"In four."

"Badgers, attack formation," I said.

The flight fanned out. We'd do a low pass strafing run, turn, drop the bombs and get out. *It should be simple*, I thought to myself.

"In three," said Maria.

I dropped us down as low as I dared. The German planes were lined up like sitting ducks beside the runway.

"Fire," I said, opening up with the cannons.

Tracers streamed out from six Mosquitos, cutting up the dirt. The German planes exploded. We didn't have time to admire the sight. We were over it and past the base.

"Bombing run," I said, turning tightly, keeping the formation.

We would fly over the field and drop the bombs as close to the main building as we could. As we approached the airbase again, tracers erupted from machine-gun emplacements.

"Incoming fire," said Jennifer.

"Badgers, stay on target," I replied.

Searchlights came on but we were over the field by then. As the Tower loomed up, I gave the order.

"Bombs away."

All six Mosquitos dropped their load. Tracers zipped past the canopy but fortunately none of them hit.

"Full throttle, Badgers, let's get the hell out of here," I said, accelerating away.

As I opened her up, we streaked across the landscape. The beach rushed by beneath us. Then we were out to sea.

"Badger Leader, there's only five of us," said Dorothy.

"Say again?" I said, looking left and right to see for myself.

"There's only five planes," Dorothy repeated.

Sure enough, she was right.

"Who's missing? Check in," I said.

The others checked in with their call signs, all except Sandra, who was Badger Five. I eased back on the throttle.

"What are you doing?" said Maria.

"I want to know where she is," I told her. "Did anyone see Badger Five go down?" I asked the others.

The response came back negative.

"Any explosion from Badger Five? Anything at all?" I asked again.

It was still negative. Sandra hadn't radioed for help or to say that she'd been hit. I wondered what the hell had happened. There was no protocol for this; we had not anticipated it. As it was, the French coast was rapidly receding behind us.

"Badger Five, do you read me?" I said over the radio.

There was no answer, so I tried again.

"Badger Five, this is Badger Leader, report in."

Still nothing.

"Perhaps she has gone down," said Maria. "Perhaps it was so sudden she couldn't radio us."

If there was no sign of Sandra's plane and no radio contact, there wasn't much I could do. I reluctantly made the decision to order the flight home.

"I've got radar contact," said Shelly suddenly. "Behind us."

I had been about to open up the throttle but stayed my hand.

"It must be her," I said. "Give us a heading. We will intercept it."

Maria looked at me but held her peace. I was in command, after all, and she rarely questioned my decisions. Shelly gave us a bearing and I turned the flight back towards the French coastline.

I knew it was dangerous; after all, it could have been a Jerry night fighter, but something told me it wasn't.

"Possible Bogie is flying in circles," said Shelly.

I grinned at Maria. "That's got to be Sandra," I said.

Maria rolled her eyes and sighed. It wasn't long before we came upon a Mosquito, emerging from the darkness.

"Badger Five, respond," I said.

There was no answer. However, it seemed as if Sandra had seen us because she turned towards us.

"All right, Badgers," I said. "Let's go home."

Making sure Sandra was definitely with the flight this time, we made our way towards the English coast.

I wondered why Sandra hadn't answered her radio but assumed there must have been a fault with it. We would find out soon enough when we landed. I put my mind back on the job.

"There they are," said Maria as we zipped over Stonehenge once more.

"They'll still be there when we're long gone, too," I mused.

"I'm not planning to be long gone for some time," said Maria firmly.

I smiled. I didn't know a crew member who went out without optimistically expecting to return. There was no other way to be. It was surprising how easily you could get used to danger and being shot at.

Hawberry airfield came into view. I lined the Mosquito up for an approach.

"Badger Leader requesting clearance," I said to Control.

"You're clear," Control replied.

The runway lights came on and we landed shortly afterwards. I taxied to our standing and killed the engines, and we jumped down through the hatchway. As we did so, I saw Sandra come running up to us.

"I'm sorry, Boss," she said when she arrived.

"What happened?" I asked her.

"My radio was hit over the airbase. We lost contact and then we didn't know exactly where we were or which way to go," she said. "Thank goodness you came after us."

"Lucky we picked you up on the radar," I said. "Otherwise, we would have headed for home."

Her face fell on hearing this. "Oh…"

"Next time, head north," said Maria. "That will get you out of enemy territory and headed back to England."

"Yes, yes, you're right," said Sandra. "That's what we should have done."

"You know the rules as well as I do," I told her. "We're supposed to keep going, no matter what."

"Yes," she said. "But you didn't…"

"Because she cares about you, you nincompoop. She cares about all of us," said Maria in admonishing tones.

"Just don't expect it every time," I added. "You need to keep it together when you're in a jam, all right?"

"Yes, I'm sorry."

"Don't be sorry," I said. "Be sensible."

Sandra looked so abashed that Maria put her arm around her shoulders.

"Come on, I think we could all use a hot cup of cocoa and a sandwich."

We walked to the truck where the others were waiting.

CHAPTER SIXTEEN

Two days later, another briefing was called just after lunch. We filed into the briefing room and waited.

"What is it this time?" said Shelly.

"Maybe Laxington is coming back for another visit," said Patricia.

"Don't joke about things like that, for Christ's sake," said Jennifer. "We had our fill of him last time."

Before anyone could reply, James, Gloria, Henry and the Marx Brothers swept into the room. As usual we stood to attention and waited for James to tell us to be at ease.

"You'll be glad to know," he said, "that we've got another mission lined up."

There was dead silence on hearing this and he seemed rather taken aback.

"Come on," he chided. "Don't all look like that — this is the big one, the one you've all been waiting for."

That made us sit up and take notice.

"I'll let my colleagues from MI6 give you the details."

This was the Marx Brothers' cue. They simultaneously stubbed out their cigarettes before stepping forward as one.

"You've no doubt heard of the Kriegsmarine," Harpo began.

"The German Navy, to be precise," added Chico, "who happen to have their headquarters in Rouen. In a chateau, no less, not far from the port."

"Yes," said Harpo. "The Kriegsmarine top brass are living it up in style."

I glanced at Maria when he said this. Hawberry Hall could hardly be designated a hovel.

"We've information that most of the Kriegsmarine High Command will shortly be gathered there for some sort of shindig," said Chico.

"Your job will be to flatten it to the ground with all of them in it, thus striking a significant blow against the Nazi regime."

Henry stepped forward on the podium. "You might ask," he said, "why we don't send a large bombing raid over there to do the job instead, and it would be a very valid question."

I *had* been wondering that myself, so I was glad that Henry had brought it up.

"There are a number of reasons, but the most cogent of these is that Jerry will see us coming for miles and by the time the bombers get there, the various brass will be sheltering from the raid, thus defeating the object." He paused for effect. "Stealth is what's needed, and stealth is what you are particularly good at. Flying in under the radar and taking the target by surprise."

He motioned to the projectionist at the back of the room and the lights were dimmed. A slide appeared on the projection screen, showing the chateau in question. It was a beautiful building, built from red and light-coloured brick with a sharply sloping roof.

"Yes, I know," said Henry, reading our thoughts. "It seems a shame to reduce it to rubble, but unfortunately the exigencies of war demand it."

He signalled to the projectionist again and an aerial photograph of the site appeared on the screen.

"You will enter enemy territory somewhere between Dieppe and Saint-Valery-en-Caux. From there it's a straight run down, mainly over rural farmland. It's fortunate that the approach to the site isn't over too much of the city, because you'll be coming in at rooftop height."

The chateau was approached via a long avenue and stood practically on its own. It would not be an easy target to miss.

"You'll fly in three planes at a time, drop and go, timing it perfectly to stay out of the blast of the ones in front. Be in no doubt that the chateau will be heavily defended with ack-ack and machine gun emplacements. Once the first blast goes off then you'll all come under fire."

We all knew this was going to be our most dangerous mission so far. Henry continued to show us various maps and aerial photographs of the intended route and surroundings, to familiarise us with the terrain. There would be further briefings and time to go over the navigation beforehand. The lights came up when he had finished.

"You will need a lot more practice flying an eighteen-plane formation," he said. "And also, the bombing run."

This all seemed straightforward enough. However, the mission itself did seem like a tall order.

"That's the gist of it," said James, taking over once more. "The timing of this is a matter of about two weeks, so we've got a lot to do by then. I know we've all been distracted of late by other unscheduled events, but now we have to focus and get the job done. Practice schedules and so forth will be posted shortly, but that's all for now. Dismissed."

The briefing broke up with a lot of excited chatter.

"Seems a shame to destroy that building," said Patricia.

"So many nice things have been destroyed already," said Connie. "What's one more?"

"Damn Hitler," said Maria.

I was about to call them to order when Judy appeared at my elbow.

"Wing Commander wants to see you, ma'am," she said.

"Aye aye, summoned again," said Shelly with a sly grin.

"Yes, of course, I will come at once," I told Judy, glaring at the others.

"Give James my regards," said Sandra, as I followed Judy out of the room.

"Don't mind them, ma'am," said Judy when we were out of earshot and walking down the corridor to James's room.

"I try not to," I replied.

"Your secret is safe with me, ma'am, never fear," she said with a wink as she opened the door to James's office to let me in.

I stared after her as she closed the door. How many other people knew our secret, I wondered? Was it even a secret anymore?

"Penny for your thoughts?" said James, coming up to me and catching my hands in his.

"It's nothing," I lied.

He let it pass and led me to the sofa. He dropped a light kiss on my lips.

"I'm sorry I didn't tell you about the mission beforehand," he said.

"Should you have?" I replied a little heatedly.

"I thought you'd be pleased to have a decent mission to fly," he said, picking up on my tone.

"Yes, I am of course..."

"But?"

I hesitated and then took the plunge. "How long can we keep doing this?" I asked him.

"Doing what?" he said, nonplussed.

"This, you and me, together like this?"

He looked a little taken aback. "What's brought this on all of a sudden?" he asked.

I sighed. It wasn't sudden for me. I had been thinking about it for a while. "It's almost as if everyone knows and they just aren't saying," I blurted out. "The others give me knowing looks, and even Judy said that my secret was safe with her."

"Well, Judy, of course, is my adjutant —" he began.

"You mean you told her?" I interrupted him, aghast.

"No, but she will have guessed. Come on, Anna, she's not stupid."

"Of course not, but what about the others?"

"They don't know for sure; perhaps they are just putting two and two together?" he ventured.

"Oh, really!" I snapped. "That's far from helpful." I immediately felt bad for snapping at him. I leant towards him and kissed him. "I'm sorry, it's just…"

"I know, Anna, but here's an idea — I've been thinking about it for a while…" He paused and looked a little apprehensive.

"What?" I asked him, wondering where this was leading.

"What if we were to become engaged?" he said with a smile.

"What?" I stared at him.

Now he'd taken the plunge, he carried on. "Wouldn't that make things easier, to make our relationship public, as it were?"

"Yes, but marriage? That's a big step," I protested, particularly since I hadn't had time to think about it.

"Well, we don't have to get married for a long time, or not at all, if you don't want to…" He trailed off, then asked, "Don't you want to get married, eventually?"

"Well, you haven't asked me," I objected.

"Do you want me to ask you?" he countered.

"I don't know," I said lamely.

James burst out laughing. "Do you know you're just about the most impossible woman I've ever met?" he said.

"How many others have you met?" I asked, recovering my composure.

"Enough to know that you are the pinnacle of impossibility."

"That's an accolade of sorts," I said, smiling.

"Just think about it, that's all I ask," he said.

"All right, but this wasn't how I imagined being asked for my hand in marriage," I told him.

"How did you imagine it?" he asked with interest.

"Well, perhaps with a little more romance ... in the moonlight. Oh, I don't know…"

"How about we revisit this after the mission?"

"All right," I agreed, not really sure if that meant he was contemplating a proposal. I was also not certain I wanted him to propose, but now the idea had been planted in my mind it refused to leave. The talk of marriage had put a different complexion on things. It showed me he was serious.

Back in my room, Jennifer was reading a manual on bombing tactics.

"Hello," she said. "Where have you been?"

"With James," I replied, sitting down on the bed with a sigh.

"What's wrong?" she asked, putting the manual down and coming to sit beside me.

"He asked me about marrying him," I told her.

"Why, that's wonderful," said Jennifer, then, seeing my expression, added, "isn't it?"

"I don't know," I said. "And he didn't exactly ask me either; he talked about the *idea* of it."

"Oh, I see … and what did you say?"

"I said I didn't know."

Jennifer laughed. "What are you like?"

I made a face and she gave me a hug.

"I just don't know if I'm in love or not. Sometimes I think I am and it's the best feeling in the world, just like you said it would be. Other times, I'm just not sure."

"Is it that, or is it that you're afraid of what everyone will think?" Jennifer was perceptive as always.

"I just need to be sure that he's the one…"

"You will be," she said, smiling.

"But how?"

"I don't know. I just know that's how it works. Be patient. In the meantime, we've got a mission to fly."

"We do indeed."

The others came into the room unannounced as usual and there was no more time to talk. Indeed, there was very little time for musing on anything at all as we prepared for the mission.

Practice for the mission went into full swing. With eighteen planes it was decided we'd fly in three groups of six, one group behind the other.

"That way, you can keep a tight, narrow flying corridor," Henry explained as he went over the tactic. "Otherwise, you'll be spread too far out, particularly when you're that low."

I kept the two radar planes with me in the leading group. I put Linda in the rear group. She barely spoke to me these days. I wondered if it was my fault for not trying harder. However, once broken, trust was difficult to regain.

My forward group consisted of myself and Maria, Jennifer and Shelly, Patricia and Connie, Susan and Pamela, Sandra and Lucy, and Molly and Eileen. We flew trial daytime runs and then night-time runs at low-level, with the groups keeping close behind each other.

"It's all going well so far," said Henry, who had been observing some of the flying practice from a newly delivered Spitfire, which replaced the one destroyed by Sandra.

"Yes," I said. "Shall we move onto bombing runs?"

"That would be my suggestion," he said.

To carry out such a run required precision. We had to fly away from the target on the practice range in formation, split into groups of three and fly back, dropping ordnance at the correct time. The bomb fuses would be on a short delay so that the gap between the groups of three did not have to be too wide — just long enough to get clear and short enough to allow the following planes time to avoid the blast.

Henry made us work through it several times, first with dummy bombs and then with live ammunition. Two weeks flew by, and before we knew it we were sitting once more in the briefing room.

"By all reports," said James, addressing the Sirens, "you've done a great job preparing for this mission. The codename for this mission is Operation Sitting Duck."

This was greeted with laughter.

"I think you can work out why it's called that," he continued. "Some of our mission planners have a sense of humour. We've been reliably informed that the Kriegsmarine Commanders will be gathered for a few days at their Rouen HQ. Based on that intelligence, the operation is scheduled for tomorrow night. I will hand you over to Henry to give you the final details."

Henry stepped forward and went over the timings and other essential matters. Mission sheets were issued with codenames, timings, waypoints and bearings for the navigators. We would have time to study all the reconnaissance photographs and maps too, which were now on the walls of the room.

As the briefing drew to a close, I wondered how tough this mission would be. It was highly likely the chateau would be heavily defended. The latest aerial reconnaissance had revealed a lot of gun emplacements, particularly surrounding the building. The port even more so, plus the naval ships had onboard anti-aircraft guns too.

"It's quite the mission we've got," said Sandra later, when our group was assembled in my room.

"Don't get too excited about the prospect of being killed," said Maria dryly.

"But it's exhilarating," Sandra protested. "It's the most excitement I've ever had."

"You have a strange idea of excitement," said Patricia, laughing.

"Why, what's yours?" Sandra asked her.

"Sitting by the fire with my feet up and a cup of tea," came the rejoinder.

We all laughed at this.

"You British are so strange," said Sandra. "You all seem so calm compared to us Americans."

"That's because we are," Connie put in. "Most of the time."

"But you're all here, fighting this war. You're all flying into danger," said Sandra, trying to fathom the British psyche.

"You're right," said Maria. "We're here because none of us can stand the thought of Britain becoming part of the Third Reich."

"And because flying a Mosquito is damn fun," Jennifer added.

"I knew it!" said Sandra triumphantly.

As I listened to them, my mind drifted. I didn't like to think that some of us might not come back from the mission, that we might not all be together again. We were a team, a unit, sisters. What would happen when the war ended, and we went our separate ways? I didn't like to think about it, because in spite of the danger, the Sirens had become my life. I didn't want that to end.

CHAPTER SEVENTEEN

The day of the mission dawned fine with a light breeze. It seemed as if flying conditions would be good that evening. The forecast confirmed it. Once we were dressed in our flying gear, James held a final briefing.

"Sirens," he said, "I want to wish you the very best of luck. You've trained hard for this mission — the importance of which cannot be stressed enough — and nobody could ask for more. I know you'll do your job and do it well." He looked around at the sea of faces. "But more importantly, do your best to come back. It's been a privilege commanding this squadron, and I want you to know how much respect I have for each and every one of you."

He glanced at me when he said it. We'd said goodbye in private beforehand. I had felt a little tearful. It was a feeling I'd not had when saying goodbye before. I hoped that it wasn't an omen.

"Come back to me, Anna," he had said.

"I'll do my best," I had replied.

It didn't seem enough of a goodbye, but the words both of us wanted to say wouldn't come out.

I forced my mind back to the present as the Marx Brothers were speaking.

"We want to wish you good luck and Godspeed," said Harpo. "Of all the squadrons we work with, this is one of the finest in the RAF. You get the job done with ruthless efficiency, and that's what's needed in a time of war."

James nodded approvingly at these words, which no doubt echoed his own sentiments. They were the kind of words you needed to hear when going into combat.

Henry and Gloria wished us well, and then it was time to go. We filed out to the waiting trucks. Connie sat at the back with Jennifer, as usual, sharing a last cigarette.

"Still excited?" Maria asked Sandra.

"Oh yeah, I really am," Sandra replied.

"We'll make a Brit of you yet," said Connie. "Then you'll learn to contain your excitement with a stiff upper lip."

We all laughed at her impersonation of a posh accent. Sandra had been a colourful addition to the squadron. Now that I was used to her ways, I wouldn't change her for the world.

The trucks arrived at the airfield and everyone assembled around me.

"All right, Sirens," I said. "You know what we've got to do. We've practised it, we've trained for it, and now let's get it done."

There was a brief cheer and then we dispersed to our various planes.

"Spoken like a proper leader," said Maria as we walked towards our Mosquito.

"Oh? Wasn't I a proper leader before?"

"You've always been a proper leader, you just didn't know it," she said.

I tucked my arm in hers affectionately for a moment. I wondered what I would do without her. It wouldn't be the same with another navigator. We climbed into the Mosquito and strapped in. I took a deep breath.

"Ready?" I asked Maria.

"Ready as I'll ever be," she replied.

I fired up the engines and when they were purring nicely, I had the rest of the flight check in before setting forth.

"Falcons, check in," I said.

Falcons had been chosen as our codename for the mission. I rather liked it, recalling the beautiful birds of prey soaring over the fields at the farm in Sussex — a life which now seemed far away. My father had always expected Jennifer and I to take over from him, but if I married James, I might never go back there. He had a career in the Air Force.

"Are you ready to go?" asked Maria, cutting into my thoughts.

"What? Yes, sorry." I put my mind back on the job at hand. Over the radio, I said, "Control, this is Falcon Leader requesting clearance."

"You're clear to go, Falcon Leader," said Control. "Good luck, stay safe out there."

"Roger," I said, smiling.

"Falcons, we're green to go," I said and eased the Mosquito out of our standing.

Seventeen Mosquitos followed suit. One by one we were airborne. As soon as we were ready, I gave the command.

"Falcons form up, close formation, low level," I said, dropping down to hedge-hopping height.

The flight split into three groups of six planes, with my group in the lead. My attention was on the terrain as I opened up the throttle. Now it was all about watching for obstacles, with Maria calling them out.

"Lines."

"Got it."

"House."

"Seen it."

We flew past Chelmsford, then east of London, crossing the Thames at Tilbury. Below us, the black hulks of ships moved slowly along the river, heading out to sea.

Maria gave us a new heading as we took a course past Chatham, towards Hastings, where we would cross the Channel.

"Do you think we'll ever get to Tunbridge Wells?" said Maria as we passed the town, reminding me of an earlier conversation concerning a Sirens outing.

"Yes, I promised we'd go, didn't I?" I replied.

"If we make it through the war, I'll hold you to it," she said with a light laugh.

"There's no *if*," I said. "We're going to make it."

"As long as you look out for that house... Watch out!"

"I've got it," I said, neatly hopping up over the building that had just appeared.

"It's won't be Jerry that kills me," quipped Maria. "It'll be a cardiac arrest."

We both laughed. It eased the tension of the flight, which was the best part of an hour to the target.

Shortly afterwards we flew over Bodiam Castle and then changed the bearing again, aiming for the coast.

"Always fancied myself as a proper princess in one of those," said Maria as the ruin slipped by below us.

"You want to live in a castle?" I said, laughing.

"Not really, too bloody draughty. I'll settle for a cottage in Wales."

The beach loomed up ahead of us between Fairlight Cove and Hastings — a pale strip of sand with the ink-black water beyond. In moments we were over the Channel. I killed the navigation lights.

The sea was calm and flat. It was a clear night and although we kept our eyes peeled for bandits, with two radar planes, I felt confident that any contact would be picked up early on.

We headed for Dieppe, aiming to make landfall just east of the town. The Channel was clear of shipping, though we had to keep a weather eye out. At the height we were flying, we could have easily run into the side of a large cruiser or merchant vessel.

Within a short while, the French coastline appeared. We passed over the beach and then we were flying low over rural France. A network of fields flashed by beneath us on the way to the target.

"Party Time in twenty," said Maria. Party Time was the codename for the target.

"Roger," I replied.

I was about to order the flight into attack formation when visibility started to deteriorate rapidly.

"What's that?" said Maria.

"Looks like a fog bank," I said as we got closer.

Moments later we were enveloped in a thick fog that seemed to have come out of nowhere. At low level, we couldn't risk hitting something. I reacted quickly.

"Falcons, we're going to five hundred feet," I said.

The entire flight gained height, but the fog was still dense.

"I can't see a damn thing," I said, my heart thumping as I strained to see anything through the fog.

There was nothing for it. The entire mission was now in jeopardy.

"Falcons, go to one thousand," I said, pulling up on the stick again.

To my relief, as we hit a thousand feet, the fog bank cleared. At least we could see the way forward. The only problem was that the fog stretched for miles, obscuring the target.

"Damn," I said. "We can't attack in this."

"What are we going to do?" asked Maria.

I thought rapidly. It was impossible to mount a stealth attack from this height. The target wasn't visible, so there was no use trying to bomb it. It seemed we had no choice. We'd have to try again another day.

"We'll have to abort," I said with a sigh.

Just then, without warning, the air exploded around us. At one thousand feet we'd been detected by enemy radar, and now the flak batteries had opened up. We were in deep trouble.

"Get us out of here," I said to Maria, then, over the radio, "Falcons abort, I repeat, abort."

Maria gave out the bearing and I banked sharply, along with the rest of the flight.

"Falcons, full throttle," I said, opening the Mosquito up to maximum.

Great puffs of smoke blew up around us, the explosions lighting up the sky. The flak was heavy, and we couldn't avoid the shards of metal winging towards us. There was nothing we could do but weather it.

Suddenly, there was a ping from the fuselage.

"Damn it, I've been hit," cried Maria.

"What?" I glanced back. Maria was clutching her leg.

"A piece of flak has hit my leg… Damn, damn!"

"Maria, get it out for goodness' sake. Get a dressing on it," I told her, feeling helpless. I couldn't exactly leave the controls.

"I'm trying… I've got it…" She let out a scream of agony.

"Maria! Don't you bloody well die on me, do you hear me?" I shouted at her.

"I'm not going to bloody well die!" she shouted back, reaching for the medical kit. "It just that bloody well hurt!"

There were more grunts and groans while she bandaged the wound as best she could before she sat back.

"Fortunately, it didn't hit an artery," she said.

I reached across to grab her hand. "Please don't die," I said. "I need you."

"I didn't know you cared," she said, smiling weakly. "Just give me a minute and I'll be all right."

I flew on, holding her hand with one hand and flying with the other. The barrage was relentless. The fog below us seemed endless. We couldn't go any lower. We were now sitting ducks.

"Christ," said Maria, squeezing my hand and recovering her composure. "It's like Dante's bloody inferno out there." She turned to the hatchway next to her. "Also, there's a hole in the door."

I could feel the air blowing in.

Suddenly, the fog bank cleared. I took immediate action.

"Falcons, move to low level," I said, diving downwards with the rest of the flight.

To my relief, we left the flak behind and were once more skimming the fields. I checked in to see if any of the other planes had been damaged, and luckily it didn't appear that we'd lost anyone.

"Are you all right to navigate?" I asked Maria.

"I'll live," she said.

"I'll take that as a yes," I told her, and she laughed.

The journey back was tense. I was worried about Maria. She might have dressed her wound, but was she losing blood? I just wanted to get us home.

Since we'd been detected, I was expecting a possible intercept by night fighters. I wasn't wrong.

"This is Falcon Four, radar contact on our nine o'clock," said Pamela.

"Confirmed," said Shelly.

"How many?" I asked them.

"Looks like two, maybe three," said Shelly.

I decided there was nothing to do but carry on and see how it played out.

"Keep going, Falcons. Falcon Four, keep me posted," I said.

Hopefully we could simply evade them. I did not want to risk a dogfight, even though we'd done it before. We needed to get Maria back for medical treatment, for one thing.

"Still coming," said Pamela a few minutes later.

This was not good news.

"Let's take an evasive course, to shake them off," I said to Maria.

"Roger," she replied, and moments later we were weaving in a series of zig-zags. It would take a little longer to reach the coast that way, but it was necessary.

Time seemed to slow down while I waited for word from the radar planes. Thankfully, just then, Pamela's voice came over the radio.

"Threat receding," she said.

"Roger," I replied. "Falcons, stay on course."

I breathed a sigh of relief as we reached the French coast without further incident, and then we were over Channel. I kept flicking anxious glances at Maria, who had her eyes closed. She looked rather pale. I let her be; there was nothing to particularly concern us over the water. As we were about to make landfall, I gave her a gentle nudge.

"Maria," I said softly.

She woke with a start. "Oh God, was I asleep?"

"Yes, you were. Listen, I'm going to hand over lead navigation to Shelly," I said, expecting her to demur.

"Sure, whatever you want, Boss," she said weakly.

"Falcon Four, take over as lead navigator," I said.

"Wilco," said Jennifer.

I decided to radio ahead to Control. They would have monitored our transmissions anyway.

"Control, this is Falcon Leader, we are en route to base. Operation Sitting Duck aborted due to fog. My navigator requires urgent medical attention on landing," I said.

"Roger, Falcon Leader, will have a medic standing by," said Control.

We approached Hawberry in short order, and it was with immense relief that I felt the wheels touch down on solid ground. I taxied to the standing, where I could see an ambulance was waiting. I pulled up and killed the engines. The hatch was opened from the outside.

"Got a casualty?" said the WAAF medic.

"Right here," said Maria.

"All right, we'll have you on a stretcher in a jiffy," she told Maria.

Shortly afterwards, I spoke to Maria in the ambulance.

"You made it," I said.

"You didn't think I'd leave you, did you?" she replied with a smile.

I squeezed her hand gratefully.

"I'll see you soon," I told her, then I jumped down from the back. They closed the doors, and I watched the ambulance leave. Not long after, I was joined by the others.

"What happened to Maria?" asked Jennifer.

"She caught a piece of shrapnel in the leg. She'll be all right, though," I said.

"That's bad luck!" said Susan.

"I think our wing might be damaged," added Molly.

"We'll check over the planes tomorrow," I said. "In any case, Victoria will be onto it."

"What happens now, Boss?" said Shelly.

"We'll have to go again another night and hope it's not foggy," I told her.

"This is my fault — maybe I'm a jinx," said Sandra.

"No," I said. "You're not a jinx. Sometimes things just don't go the way we planned. Anyway, let's get back to Hawberry."

We returned in the trucks and went to the dining room. The usual refreshments were laid on. I was sipping a mug of cocoa and eating a corned beef sandwich when James appeared.

"You heard the news?" I asked him as he came up to me.

"Yes, I did. That was bad luck," he replied.

"The fog or Maria?" I couldn't help saying.

"Of course, Maria. It's a damn shame. I'm glad she made it back," he said. "The fog too, of course."

"We'll have to go again," I said before he even mentioned it.

"I'm afraid so, and in short order. We've only got a limited amount of time."

"I know," I said. "And we're ready to go, but there's some damage to the planes."

"Henry is already liaising with the ground crew," James replied. "They'll work through the night if they have to."

"So, we go tomorrow if possible?" I asked him.

"Yes, if it's possible."

"Let's hope there's no fog," I said.

The more times we attempted the mission, the more likely it was that the Germans would divine our intent. To some degree we had already lost the element of surprise.

"I hope so too."

He smiled and I could see the question in his eyes. He couldn't ask me directly if he'd see me later. Not in front of everyone.

"I've got to see Maria, first," I said softly, giving him the answer he wanted.

"Of course."

He gave me a brief formal salute. Then he lingered to say well done and bad luck to the rest of the Sirens before leaving. I finished my sandwich then made my way to the medical unit.

I had fortunately not seen much of the medical unit since I'd been with the Sirens. It was set up in a suite of rooms that had been requisitioned for the purpose. It was staffed by several nurses, a junior doctor and a senior doctor, Flight Officer Sophie Carpenter. She was around thirty years old and wore glasses. Quite complicated surgery could apparently be performed on site if needed.

"Hello," she said when I entered her domain.

"Hi," I said. "I was hoping for an update on ASO Preston?"

"Oh yes, shrapnel in the leg. Nasty wound. We've cleaned and stitched it up. We're lucky to have some penicillin; it's not widely available yet, but I managed to snag a supply a while ago. I've given her a shot of that for good measure."

"So, she's all right?" I asked her, wanting to be sure.

"She is indeed. Had it hit an artery, then she would have bled to death. Her prompt first aid, albeit self-administered, certainly helped."

This was a sobering thought.

"Thank you, Doctor," I said. Then I asked the obvious question. "Will she be fit for active duty?"

Dr Carpenter contemplated me for a moment before answering. "That depends."

"On what?"

"Well, on whether you allow her to fly and whether you can stop her from flying." She laughed. "I'd normally recommend bed rest for something like this. However, she's already informed me in no uncertain terms that she's going back out there, so…" She grinned and shrugged helplessly.

"Has she indeed?" I said, smiling. This was typical of the Maria I knew.

"Would you like to see her?"

"Yes, I would," I said.

Dr Carpenter led me down a short corridor to a room, opened the door and let me in. The room contained a bed, oxygen tanks and other medical paraphernalia. It was nicely appointed and had obviously been a bedroom or similar at one time.

"You have a visitor," Dr Carpenter said to Maria, who was sitting up in the bed.

She was holding a bowl of soup, which she set aside on a table next to the bed. The fact that she had an appetite was a good thing.

Dr Carpenter left us to it. Maria gave me a broad grin.

"How are you?" I asked her, perching on the bed beside her.

"I'm a bit sore, but I'll be right and ready to go again in the morning," she said.

"You know, the doctor says you should really rest," I told her. I couldn't resist teasing her a little, just to see her reaction.

"Well, I don't care what the doctor says. I'm going on that mission!" she said, firing up at once.

"And if I order you not to?" I said, amused.

Maria did not see the funny side and said hotly, "Then I'll disobey your order, ma'am!"

I burst out laughing and so did she.

"Silly goose," I said. "I haven't got another navigator anyway."

"Don't wind me up like that, for God's sake," Maria complained. "I really thought you were serious."

"Hardly," I replied. "I know how damn stubborn you are."

I couldn't resist giving her a hug before leaving her to get some sleep. I made my way to James's room without a second thought. It just seemed the natural thing to do.

CHAPTER EIGHTEEN

The following morning, Maria appeared at breakfast.

"Have you been discharged?" I asked her in surprise.

"I discharged myself. I wanted to eat with the gang, not in the medical unit on my own."

I glanced at her plate, which was full. "I see you haven't lost your appetite."

"It's surprising what a bit of shrapnel in the leg can do," she said, laughing.

"That was pretty crazy up there last night," said Pamela.

"Scary, more like," Susan replied.

"Now we know what the bomber crews face every time they go out," I told them.

It was a sobering thought. The casualties on daytime bombing raids were high from flak, as well as from enemy fighters. We were lucky to be flying stealth missions, without too much incoming fire.

"Are we going again, Boss?" asked Shelly.

"We are, but I have to check with Victoria and Henry regarding the state of the planes," I replied.

Maria got up to go for seconds.

"Blimey," said Shelly. "You're hungry today."

"What?" Maria threw back. "I've been shot. Give a girl a break."

We all laughed and watched her return to the serving area. I finished my eggs on toast, beans and fried spam on the side. When Maria had finished her second helping, I took her with me to the airfield in a staff car, along with Jennifer and Shelly.

We found Victoria in the main hangar working on one of the planes. She stopped what she was doing and saluted.

"I've just come to check on the state of play," I said. "How much damage was there?"

"Fortunately, not too much," she said. "A few holes, which we've patched up; we're working on that damaged wing."

"Have you been working all night?" I asked her.

"Yes, but don't worry. It will all be ready for another go tonight." Victoria produced a jagged shard of metal from her pocket and held it out to me. "That's the shrapnel from your plane — we found it on the floor of the cockpit."

I took it and examined it briefly, then handed it to Maria.

"Christ!" exclaimed Maria, turning it over in her hands.

"You were lucky," Victoria said to her.

"I suppose that providence was smiling on me last night," Maria quipped before putting the piece of shrapnel into her pocket. "I'll keep that to show my grandchildren, if I ever have any."

Victoria took us on a tour of the aircraft, showing us the repairs. There was more minor damage than I had thought, but we were lucky not to have come off worse.

We headed back to Hawberry in a sober mood.

There was no second briefing. Instead, we passed the day resting up, playing cards and chatting. As the time to get changed into our flying gear approached, I sneaked away to see James.

He was alone in his office. He got up at once when he saw me.

"Anna," he said, taking me into his embrace.

"It's nearly time to go," I replied.

"I know."

We kissed as if it would be our last.

"Take care out there," he said, eventually letting go of me.

"I will."

"Come back to me, Anna."

"I will."

This was our talisman: the same words spoken every time I left, as if they would somehow bring me luck. I returned to my room to get changed, and walked in to find Jennifer and Connie in a close embrace. Startled, they pulled apart.

"Don't mind me," I said. "We all have our secrets."

"Yes," said Connie with a meaningful look, "we do. Anyway, I've got to change."

She slid her hand out of Jennifer's and left the room.

"What did she mean by that?" I said to Jennifer.

"Nothing," said Jennifer, pulling on her flying gear.

"Does she know about me and James? Did you tell her?" I demanded.

Jennifer sighed. "You know it's going to come out in the end, Anna," she said. "Maybe it's better if it comes from you."

"I don't know what to do," I said helplessly, as I pulled on my boots. "I'm just not sure James loves me."

"Anyone with half a brain can see that he loves you," she said with a laugh.

"But I want him to say it," I told her.

"Perhaps you have to say it first? Anyway, it's time to go."

We walked downstairs, through the atrium and out to the waiting trucks. Jennifer's words stuck in my mind. Perhaps I did have to say it first. But what if he didn't say it back? Then I would look like a fool. I cursed my own naivety about love.

There was little chatter in the truck this time around. We all felt a little more tense. Connie and Jennifer were sharing a cigarette. Connie looked over at me and gave me a reassuring smile. Perhaps Jennifer had said something to her.

We arrived at the airfield, where I was met by Victoria. After exchanging salutes, she said, "They're all ready for you, ma'am. Good luck."

"Thanks," I said, then I turned to address the Sirens. "All right, Sirens, let's put yesterday behind us and get the job done this time."

With that, we boarded our aircraft and were soon heading towards the runway in procession.

"How's the leg?" I asked Maria as I got ready to open up the throttle.

"Still painful, but I'll be okay."

"All right, then let's do this."

We hurtled down the runway and were soon airborne.

I gave the command to the squadron. "Falcons, close formation, low-level flying."

We had kept the same codename, since changing it was deemed unnecessary. Then we were off, speeding over the landscape once more. The sky wasn't quite as clear as the previous night, with a few clouds scudding across the moon.

We covered the same route down past Chelmsford, east of London, across the Thames and on to Hastings.

"Do you think there'll be more fog?" Maria asked as we approached the coastline.

"I bloody well hope not," I said. "It's the last thing we need."

"We don't need another flak barrage, that's for sure," said Maria.

"If there's fog, we'll turn back rather than try to climb over it," I told her.

I wasn't risking it a second time. We might not be so lucky.

The pale line of the sandy beach flashed by beneath us and then we were over the Channel. The water was choppy. We were flying into a slight offshore breeze. I kept us a little higher on account of it. However, we passed over the water without incident and soon the French coast was upon us.

"Here we go," said Maria.

"Here we go, indeed," I replied.

It felt like déjà vu as we took the same route as the night before. The same houses, telegraph lines, trees and hedges appeared and had to be negotiated. It took all of our attention and so I had little time to think about anything else.

Time seemed to pass quickly. Then Maria broke the silence.

"Twenty minutes to Party Time and there's no fog," she said.

The way ahead was thankfully clear, so I gave the command. "Falcons, attack formation."

We once again split into three groups of six, with my group leading. The groups behind us would throttle back to attain the correct distance between us.

Maria gave us a new bearing. "Party Time in fifteen," she said.

The adrenaline was already flowing, putting me on high alert as we approached the target.

"Party Time in ten," said Maria.

I wondered when the defences would detect us and open up. With any luck, it wouldn't be until the last minute. I slipped the safety off the guns in readiness. Up ahead, I could see the black outline of houses as we approached the outskirts of Rouen.

"Party Time in five," said Maria.

I opened the bomb bay doors, then the radio crackled to life.

"Falcon Leader, this is Control, divert, I say again, divert, new primary, here are the coordinates."

I looked at Maria, who was frantically writing them down.

"Wilco," I said to Control. There was no time to ask what was going on; I had to tell the others. "Falcons, we have a new primary, not Party Time, I repeat not Party Time. Maintain formation, follow my lead."

"It's the port — they want us to attack the port," said Maria. "Stay on this line; we'll go over the top of the chateau and hit the port directly afterwards."

The chateau loomed up in front of us, sticking out like a sore thumb. It was indeed a sitting duck, but no longer for us. For a moment there was no incoming fire, and then tracers started flying.

"Here we bloody well go," said Maria.

"Stay on course, Falcons," I said. "Drop on my mark."

I pulled up and over the chateau and throttled up towards the port, which was dead ahead.

Streams of tracers shot past us, but luckily none of them hit us. Searchlights came on at the port defences. They started scanning the sky, trying to catch us in their beams. There wasn't time to change formation, although it would have made more sense to get an even bomb coverage. Since our presence was now known, I gave the others the new mission.

"Falcons, the port is our primary. Pick your own target. Let's get a good spread."

Heavy ack-ack guns opened up from the ships. I kept flying, my heart in my mouth. The ships had far more firepower, and they were using it to full effect. Moments later, the port was beneath us.

"Bombs away," I said, releasing the ordnance. We flew a little further south as the explosions went off behind us. I followed the course of the river to avoid flying over the city itself. Maria gave the bearing to the others to go onto once they'd dropped their payload.

The second group dropped their bombs, and then the third. The sky was lit up by an enormous fireball. That would make it harder for the defenders to see the incoming planes. As the last group dropped their bombs and got clear, there was a frantic call.

"We're hit! We're hit!" It was SO Nancy Williams and her navigator, ASO Rita Parsons.

I glanced over to the right to see a plane on fire. I watched in horror as it dived down and exploded. Before I could register that, there came another call.

"We're hit. We're going down." It was SO Ruby King and ASO Kay Butler.

I looked across but could see no sign of their plane. If they had gone down, there had been no explosion.

"Falcon Three Six, what's your situation?" I asked them.

"Can't... We can't..." came the response from Ruby.

I thought quickly. I could not leave them there to be captured. There was only one thing for it.

"Falcons, Group One stay with me," I said. "Groups Two and Three, head for home. Falcon Two One can lead."

"Wilco," said SO Marilyn Henderson, flying Falcon Two One. They obeyed without question as Marilyn took over that part of the flight.

I turned our plane back towards the port.

"What are you doing?" asked Maria.

"What I have to do," I replied. "We need to find that plane."

"And then what?"

I didn't answer because Maria knew. The others in my group had formed up and followed me. I flew in the approximate direction Ruby must have gone down.

"Keep your eyes peeled for Falcon Three Six," I told the others as we skimmed low over the fields. Suddenly, the radio crackled to life.

"Falcon Leader, we're down. We can't move; Kay's been hit," said Ruby.

"Falcon Three Six, you know what you need to do," I said, unable to keep the tremor from my voice.

"I can't reach the grenade… I'm trapped… I'm sorry," came the desperate response.

"I'm sorry too, Ruby," I said. We both knew what I had to do.

"Just do it, Anna," she said. "And give my regards to Blighty."

I flicked a glance at Maria. She was looking grim. In the darkness, there was the gleam of an aircraft canopy just up ahead.

"There they are," said Jennifer. "On our twelve o'clock."

"On my command, open fire," I told them.

"You're really going to do this?" said Maria, her eyes wide.

"Do I have a choice?" I shot back.

None of us had anticipated something like this. But we were at war, and sometimes there was only one option.

"No, I suppose not," said Maria; then she fell silent.

I waited until the Mosquito was in plain sight, and then I gave the order. "Fire."

We were trained to follow orders. Nobody disobeyed. Tracers flew out from every Mosquito, raking up the dirt. They hit Ruby's plane, which burst into flames. We passed overhead and as we left it behind, the fuel tanks exploded. I was relieved that we didn't need to go in for a second run.

"Give me the bearing," I said to Maria.

"I can't believe —" she began, but I cut her off.

"Give me the bloody bearing and let's get out of here!" I shouted.

She hastily read it out.

227

I turned the plane onto the heading and throttled up. We flew in silence. I did not dare look at Maria. I dashed angry tears from my eyes. I forced my attention onto the terrain in front and tried to push the horror of my actions from my mind.

The flight back was a blur. It should have been a relief to cross the Channel once more and regain the shores of Blighty. Instead, it only brought the moment closer when I would have to face the truth. I had ordered the death of one of our own, one of the Sirens, whom I'd sworn to protect.

Finally, we made it to the airbase.

"Control, this is Falcon Leader, requesting permission to land," I said in clipped tones.

"Falcon Leader, you're clear. The rest of the flight is back already."

"Roger," I said, turning onto our approach.

We landed with a bit of a bump. With a curse, I taxied to our standing and killed the engines. I sat there, staring out into the night.

I could feel Maria's gaze upon me and her hand reached out to touch me.

"Anna," she said gently.

"What?" I whispered in a stricken voice, turning to meet her eyes. Tears streamed down my face.

"You did what you had to do, Anna. We all did."

"I killed them," I said.

"*We* killed them… We had to. If they'd been captured, then they would have suffered a much worse fate."

"I don't know if I'm fit to be Flight Leader."

"Stop it!" said Maria. "You are fit to be the leader precisely because you did what other people might not. You protected the Sirens by your actions."

I choked back the tears and wiped them away. "Let's get out of here. I need to get out of here," I told her.

"All right," she said.

She climbed out gingerly, to avoid aggravating her injured leg, and I jumped down after her. I could see the rest of the squadron approaching, but I couldn't face them just then.

"I need some time on my own," I told Maria.

I turned and strode away into the darkness towards the edge of the airfield.

"Leave her," I heard Maria saying. "She needs to be alone right now; she's a bit upset."

The landing lights had gone out and the field was in darkness. I walked right to the perimeter. There was a concrete barrier running around the edge. I sat down on it and started to sob.

I didn't know how long I had been there, but suddenly James was by my side. He took me in his arms and held me close while I cried into his jacket.

"It's all right, Anna. It's all right," he said softly.

"I've done a terrible thing," I said, pulling away.

"I heard what happened," he replied. "You did the only thing possible under the circumstances."

"If you say so," I said. "I find it hard to square it with my conscience."

"You did your duty. Sometimes that might go against everything we believe, but we still have to do it, for the greater good."

I looked up into his face. He was smiling at me.

"James," I said earnestly, "I don't know if I can do this anymore."

"Do what?" he asked.

"All of this — be the Flight Leader, be part of the Sirens. I don't know if I can do it, not after this."

"You can, Anna. You *have* to," he said. "The Sirens need you. And because..."

"Because?" I repeated, staring at him.

"Because *I* need you," he said.

"You need me?"

He sighed. "Now is probably not the time, but what the hell? I need you because I love you, Anna. That's why you can't leave."

My heart started to beat rather fast. "Oh, James," I said. "I love you too, so much..."

His lips met mine and everything else was momentarily forgotten. There would be time to talk it through. But for now, James loved me, and that was all that mattered.

HISTORICAL NOTE

As I noted above, the Mosquito squadrons were tasked with attacking German airbases in France and also the Netherlands. The stealth mode of low-level night missions made them a particular nuisance to the Luftwaffe. As the Luftwaffe got wise to it, they would also deploy their own night fighters in order to try and shoot down the allied planes. Nevertheless, the campaign was effective and that's no doubt why the allies continued with it.

High level bombing was also employed, but the bombers could be seen coming for miles on radar and planes could be scrambled, thus leaving less of a target. Sustained bombing of runways was also carried out in order to disable airbases.

As I also said, the Kriegsmarine had their French HQ in a chateau at Rouen. The chateau still stands today and is part of the Rouen Business School. It once stood on its own up a long a driveway, but now, of course, it's surrounded by other buildings that are all part of the Business School. One of the Kriegsmarine's main missions was to disrupt allied shipping and in particular convoys travelling across the Atlantic with supplies from America. Naturally a chance to decimate their high command would be one the allies would have taken, had the opportunity actually arisen to do so.

Returning to the history of women in combat: the truth is that women in the British forces were not allowed to engage in combat. This would have required an act of Parliament or the amendment of an act of Parliament, which was unfortunately probably a bridge too far for some MPs. However, it brought up some situations which seem ludicrous in hindsight. For example, women worked on the ack-ack batteries and were known to be excellent at range-finding, aiming the guns and so forth, but they were never actually allowed to fire the guns. This always required a man to do it. While that might certainly seem absurd now, it was part of the mores of the time. This also meant that women in the British forces did not carry arms, fire weapons and more, unlike, for example, in the Soviet Union, where women were proficient in the use of weapons; battalions of women fought against the Germans on the field of combat. So, in reality, women were constrained in that way in British and American forces. It was fine for women to do everything but fight.

I think it's partly that incongruous situation which led me to invent the Sirens. Had British women been allowed to fight, I am sure they would have acquitted themselves just as well as my fictional squadron, if not better. One wonders what would have happened had the Germans invaded Britain. I am sure that women would have taken up arms.

In case it's thought that the invention of Air Commodore Laxington and his antipathy towards the Sirens might be a little farfetched, it should be noted that the editor of *Aeroplane* magazine once wrote about the Air Transport Auxiliary:

We quite agree that there are millions of women in the country who could do useful jobs in the war. But the trouble is that so many of them insist on doing jobs which they are quite incapable of doing. The menace is the woman who thinks that she ought to be flying a high-speed bomber when she really has not the intelligence to scrub the floor of a hospital properly.

This was penned when the ATA decided to appoint eight specially selected women to transport planes. The pressure of war and the loss of male pilots meant that many more swelled their ranks over time, transporting all kinds of planes including high-speed fighters and bombers. In America, there were true stories of the WASPS being harassed by men who thought they shouldn't be flying planes. The men's offences included putting sugar in the fuel tanks of planes the women were about to fly. Sadly, some women fliers in the WASPS did perish.

Although the Sirens never existed, in my mind such a squadron should have been put together. I'm glad to have been able to bring that thought to life.

A NOTE TO THE READER

Dear Reader,

In this second episode of the Sirens, I wanted to explore the maturing of their experiences in combat and out of it. Any squadron would get depleted over time by losses and it was obvious that more pilots and navigators would be needed, particularly if it was successful. It also meant I could introduce some interesting new characters to the fold.

One of the things I most enjoy about writing these books is the banter and the light touches of humour. Although war is a serious business, the British way of getting through adversity is by having a laugh or two. So it's very much true to form.

Adding in an American pilot made sense to me and changed the dynamics again. Sandra definitely became one of my favourite characters, along with those already in the series.

Not all the missions actually happened, although Mosquito squadrons were heavily involved in night attacks on airbases during World War Two. The Kriegsmarine HQ was at Rouen in a chateau, though it was never officially attacked.

The life of any squadron was also not simply flying missions. In my books I like to weave in the other aspects of their lives, the inevitable ups and downs. If I've managed to capture a snapshot of what might have been and made an interesting or entertaining story out of it, then I've done my job.

I hope you enjoyed reading this novel as much as I enjoyed writing it. If you did, then I would be very grateful if you could spare the time to write a review on **Amazon** and **Goodreads**. As an author, these reviews are hugely important, and always appreciated.

You can connect with me in other ways too, via my **website**, **Facebook**, **Twitter**, **Instagram**, and a special **Secret Sirens Page.**

I very much hope you were entertained enough to read the next book in the Sirens series.

Warmest regards,

D. R. Bailey

Sapere Books is an exciting new publisher of brilliant fiction and popular history.

To find out more about our latest releases and our monthly bargain books visit our website:
saperebooks.com